LOVE ON THIN ICE 3 - HEALING

This is a work of fiction. Names, characters, places and incidents either are the product of the author's imagination or are used fictitiously. Any resemblance to actual persons, living or dead, events, or locales is entirely coincidental.

Copyright © 2022 by Vallean Jackson

All rights reserved. No part of this book may be reproduced or used in any manner without written permission of the copyright owner except for the use of quotations in a book review. For more information, email: authorvalleanj@gmail.com

Book cover design: Nubian FX Covers & design
Published by VX Publishing LLC
www.valleanj.com

Dedication

I dedicate this book to every King & Queen that has experienced love, but it didn't turn out how you expected it to. Just know what seems like a failed relationship isn't your end, learn from what could have broken you, and try again. Every relationship isn't meant to be forever. Some are used for your own personal growth, and getting a better version of you is sometimes the best outcome of the whole ordeal.

Don't take old hurt into a new relationship. If you do, the outcomes will likely be the same or worse, and lastly, do not talk yourself out of love for you are worthy of being loved!

Find that love that helps you develop into your best self. Brush yourself off and get back in the ring! This go around might just be the win you've always dreamed!

~ **Author Vallean J.**

One year later......

CHAPTER 1

Keiontay

In the time frame of a year, so much can happen and change. For my life that is an understatement. I managed to land on my feet, barely. A day later or a minute too late and I would have probably been in a casket instead of the chance to get my life together. I have not figured it all out, but I have taken the initiative to start. When you reach the point where life puts you at a crossroad and you make it out alive, second chances make you want to change and add some value to your life. That was my problem, I was living but was not adding value to my life. Instead I was constantly taking away from myself, feeling almost untouchable and spreading myself way too thin. I can't point any fingers when it all points back to me.

To blame my upbringing, and people that let me get away with things is a cowardly, and narrow minded way of thinking. Yet it's my truth. I feel like with the stuff I saw growing up, a child truly should not see but too often it is not addressed and brushed under the rug. This usually leads to a lot of kids including myself growing up before their time, losing their childhood early and having to step into adulthood. The worst part is seeing shit and figuring out what you saw, and how to get over something you do not even understand. My mother and father, the foundation of your growth, your parents... mine really fucked me up. To see my mother and father fighting like cats and dogs is mentally and emotionally disturbing. As a kid, I stood there and watched the days my father would get drunk. Him and my mom would fight because he couldn't control his alcohol or temper. The slightest thing like my mom asking if he had been drinking all night usually led to him hitting her, depending on the day. My mom being this strong woman for me when she was probably broken inside really fucks with me because I couldn't help her. Then there was a time when I did not know who side to take because they both were my parents.

The shit is crazy and then my father went to jail when I was around ten years old for selling cocaine. His imprisonment created a gap in my life where I had to use my surroundings to help me grow into a man. I had to step up and be the man of the house, you know almost the typical black male story of being raised by a single mother. I hated that my father couldn't be more responsible and selfless.

I used to see my parents go to work, hold shit down, and one day it all seemed to blow up. I stood and watched everything fall to pieces. Like any kid I loved both of my parents, but my father's absence really made me angry because he could have made better decisions so he could have been there for my mother and I. He could have left the streets and continued to work like he was but he got greedy. My father was on a roll with owning his own business, but fucked it up because he started mixing business with pleasure and I ain't talking sex. He found out some of his employees liked to get high off coke, and he saw it as a double win.

He was paying them to work and in return they were spending the money they earned back to him for cocaine. My father saw it as the perfect come up, but sometimes a good thing can quickly turn sour and that is what happened. His greed gave him the big head and made him feel like the head honcho. He wanted to be like the damn Godfather and have people coming to the house for pickups and my mother was not having it. That is something else they fought about. She wanted him to stop selling drugs, continue working in construction, and just be a family man. But he fought with her verbally and physically. Then outside of the arguing and fighting, I think the worst shit of it all was the day my mother called the police and sent my father up the road. She had had enough. Between the domestic violence cases they had accumulated, assault charges from when he was younger, and now to add drugs to the list landed my father a hefty fifteen years behind bars. My mother refused to get him a lawyer because she said she was tired. She admitted to my father of being the one to snitch on him selling drugs, and until this very day she does not regret her decision.

She might not regret it, but their choices and decisions left me fucked up, and damn near almost repeating their mistakes because they could not fix them then. That is that generational curse shit for you right there and I didn't even realize it until I had time to just reflect on my life. Like so much anger and confusion is bottled up because while my father was away my mother held shit down for us, and I respect that. She never dropped the ball, we were always straight so I have much respect for that and will always love my mother for her sacrifices. So when it comes to some shit going down in my life I reach out to my mother cause I know without a doubt my mother has my back. My father, his absence felt intentional. We never went to see him, he never wrote really, and when he did the letters were short. Almost like he gave up so that made me feel worse. He could have called at least once a month, or wrote a full letter. I wanted to know how he was and tell him about what was going on, but his lack of interest led me to believe he didn't care. With me reaching out to him, it was a waste of time so I didn't. Now that he has done his time and is back in the house with my mother, there is some disconnect. As if there is an elephant in the room that no one wants to address. Some days I feel like he doesn't want to be there, he is still angry, or he simply does not give a shit so the relationship isn't too strong between us.

When I was a teenager, I used to wish my father could attend my games, that I could share my stories with him, get advice from him, just have his help in general but that was nonexistent. I had to learn to do without. So no, I did not see the proper way of how to treat a woman. How is a man supposed to do the right thing and be accountable? I saw all the wrong shit and it seems like that is unfortunately the man I am growing into and I hate that shit. I want to be nothing like my father because he could have made better choices. His and I relationship is like one someone would have with their neighbor. We speak, say a few words, and then go on about our business. He gives his input here and there, but a lot of times it goes in one ear and out of the other.

Like who the fuck are you to give me some advice. I am making these fucked up decisions from watching the bullshit he did. Even though I have fought like hell to be everything he was not, I am unfortunately following in his footsteps. I am at the point I am mad at myself. I walked out on my son and the woman I love, because she wanted better for me and I fought against that. As if she was not supporting me when she only wanted the best for me but I couldn't see that then. So used to having my way that I was willing, hell did walk out on the woman I finally fell in love with, for the first time in my life. Before going to Nova after those two months I should have done what my mother suggested that day and got back on the plane, and fixed the chaos I had caused. However, she gave me an out that I could stay home for a little bit until I got my mind together. So instead of rushing back, that is what I did to get my mind together.

I saw no need in rushing back to fix things when mentally I wasn't ready. I felt heart broken, betrayed, stupid, stressed, frustrated and a whole bunch of other shit. To find out Kaleigh was not my daughter was something that had me on my knees talking to God. It is always good to pray but I had long ago fallen short of praying to the man above. Finding out about Kaleigh felt like I had been shot or like I was grieving the loss of my child. Then the one person I would talk to about all this shit would have been Tarven, but I can't now because he knew the truth all along but never told me because he too wanted to hurt me. Shit sounds like some bitch shit, but he was in on the shit just like Ginger. For me it was double the betrayal and how to process that is something I don't even know how to begin. I thought about counseling, but in all honesty I didn't feel like being bothered or talking to anyone. Over the course of those two months while staying at my parent's house, I stayed in my room honestly. Didn't do shit but play the game. I barely ate. I slept most of the day, kept the shades down and the curtains closed. I just wanted the world blocked out and that's what I did. My mother tried to talk to me here and there, and my father even came in to try and be understanding, but the pain I was feeling felt like nobody would understand.

A part of me wanted to die because I felt so foolish, but knowing I have a living and biological son gave me a reason to want to live. With the belief that I could get me together enough to be there for him as best I could. Thinking about Nolan made me depressed too because I missed so much of his life already fucking around with Ginger, letting her lies and deception plague my mind. There is some stuff that is hard to get over and the shit Ginger and Tarven did to me really is unforgivable. I shouldn't have gone back to Nova so soon, but I felt like if I made it back to her and spent time with my son I could be whole again. I did not account for the fact that in order for me to be whole again, I first had to address what felt like was broken in me. Plus that was a reality that was unlikely to happen when I had hurt the one woman I actually loved, and that too somehow truly fuck me up too. I was trying to hold it in the road while I was there, but the arguing and her just not falling back into my arms like nothing happened made me angry.

Like I know I fucked up but love me anyway. Then when we started back having sex, I felt like I had my foot back in the door. To hear she didn't want to just be back into a relationship with me was a trigger of rejection. Almost like she was betraying me too and that made me angry.

The minute I reached out to Malachi to help me get back on my feet was the first step of a wrong decision. I was stubborn and pig headed in my actions. Of course he saw that and was more than willing to help me sink myself. The day I went to pick up the pills ruined any chances of bonding with the woman I love and being a father.

She wanted me to just take the time and do the right thing, go the blue collar route and build towards my dreams. She was more than willing to support that choice, but she said selling pills was me short cutting the man I truly could be. At the time things got heated and my passion to want to make money and declare I am a man and could hold shit on my own that I couldn't see she was right. I told this woman if I left out the door I would never look back, even changed my number and blocked her on what little social media I did have just in case she tried to even reach out. Why? Because I was mad. I didn't feel like she was understanding where I was coming from and why I needed to do this. I even explained that I had no intentions of doing it for long but she was not hearing that. I felt like she was being selfish and inconsiderate.

However, at no point did I inform her of why I felt like I needed to do this. I just expected her to read my mind like most people do when shit is bothering them, but don't want to talk about it. The truth was, I wanted to sell and be in the streets because I knew the streets could make you hard. The streets bring out the man in you whether you are ready or not because if there's any bitch in you, the streets will reveal that, and I needed my ego reconstructed. I needed to feel like a man. Well a depiction of what I used to see as a man. Because after the day Ginger confirmed that Kaleigh was not my daughter that truly fucked me up. Then finding out they were basically black mailing Nova cause she found out did something to me, and for the father to be a dude I thought of as my brother, my best friend; man that shit righteously had me feeling empty. Empty and angry. But a part of me still wanted love because I also felt broken.

For so many years, I felt obligated to be around Ginger because of the shit she did for me and she sat on that phone and laughed damn near as she explained how she knew from the jump Kaleigh was not my kid. Like she had me going to appointments with her, baby shower, in the delivery room holding her hand and everything, trying to be with her every step of the way and just like that it was all a lie. I know I might seem like I am all over the place but the shit that happened to me last year damn near had me about to end my life. Finding out Kaliegh was not my daughter felt like a piece of me had died and I was not sure how to revive myself. I mean every step of the way, I wanted to be involved in this little girl's life. I did the skin to skin so we could have our own bond, walked the floor with her as a newborn, hell I even fucked up the relationship with the girl of my dreams just to be by her side. I wanted the best for her so much that I used to sleep in her crib so Ginger would not hurt her because she couldn't stand how much I protected Kaleigh. I knew my relationship with Kaleigh bothered her, but I was a proud dad who could blame me. Or so I thought. Like mentally I just remember the threats and some of the threats being played out of putting Kaleigh in the dryer or leaving her in the car. The times she threatened to drop her because she was mad at me. She knew that by messing with her I would bow down gracefully.

I stayed to protect her basically and she knew that, and I don't regret protecting her to this day but it hurts like hell that I no longer am her protector. I am sad to not be able to further be a part of her life, but a piece of me does feel free from the weight of Ginger. Ginger brought so much hell into my life. Time after time I made excuses for her, and now I don't have that problem which feels like a breath of fresh air. However, I feel selfish because there is no telling how she will treat her now since I am not around. But I can't go back, I need to be trying to figure out how to find my way back to Nova and Nolan but maybe I shouldn't be around Nolan or even deserve to be around him, how fucked up I am. I don't want to ruin him. I don't want him to see his mother and I argue. I don't know what to do because either way I look at it I don't seem to fit in his life, and with Nova I did her so unnecessarily wrong she probably will never talk to me again. It's so much I need to get straight.

Oh I think I forgot to mention that I am in the hospital recovering from a deal gone bad. I went to deliver some pink Lortabs to one of the old ladies that had become one of the regulars, and she snuck me. Never in a million years did I think Ms. Nikki would have pulled some shit like that. She said she was taking the pills because her insurance would not cover her full prescription so she had to do what she had to do to not be in pain. I never suspected she was abusing the meds. I guess it went from managing pain to managing her addiction. I don't know, but when I showed up to deliver, I called her to come out to the car, she said she couldn't make it out because she was hurting too bad so I went to the door to make the exchange. When she opened the door, and I handed her the pills she handed me her money but asked for change back. I thought that was weird because she had given the exact amount of $200 so I just ignored it. Before I knew it, as I looked down in my pocket to count the money she had given me of $20 dollar bills to make sure I was not tripping, she stabbed me in the middle of my stomach right there in her doorway. Damn near sending me to my knees.

Of course she didn't stop there. As I tried to stand up to gain my balance, I saw a fist coming at me knocking me back on my ass as I tried to hold my wound. All I could make out was that the guy was dark skinned and looked to have dreads but I was not fully sure as he punched me in my face again causing my nose to bleed. As I turned to my side to lay in the fetal position, I could feel being stabbed in my right hip that had me screaming out for dear life. I could feel one of them going in my pockets and taking the same money Ms. Nikki had just given me and tried to go in my other pocket but I applied as much pressure as I could so they couldn't. That shit made me so angry that my adrenaline kicked in and I was able to gain the strength to drag my body to my car. They had closed the door and left me on the porch to die and every second I drug my body to try and fight for my life. I contemplated giving up, but I refused to die there. As I made it to my 2019 black and red Chevrolet Camaro LT, I found a shirt in my back seat, tied it around my hip wound as quickly as I could with one eye closed. Only God knows how I made it to the hospital but all I know is that when I looked out of my left eye I saw the emergency sign, put the car in park, and all I remember is my head hitting the horn. Then me waking up in this hospital bed.

CHAPTER 2

Nova

It has been a year and some change since the day Keiontay walked out and he has held to his word of not looking back. I really never wanted things to get to that point with us. I felt that even if we couldn't work out that we could at least co-parent, but that's nonexistent. That day he left, he blocked me from phone calls to social media. Any possible way that I could contact him, he cut off. I even tried calling from another number, until I realized he had changed his number. This new level of anger and shutting me out had me filled with a roller coaster of emotions and insecurities. It was now to the point that I questioned if I was girlfriend material and if the problem was really me and didn't know it. I know I have some issues of my own, but I just thought the love in me to give was greater but I see it was not enough. I started to question my beauty and my weight. Maybe that could be the problem. Was my beauty fading to him, or maybe it was the weight I gained from carrying Nolan.

I did gain like twenty five to thirty pounds, and I am not just saying its baby weight cause my ass has been eating. Between emotional eating and sometimes just being too tired to cook, fast food and junk food has become my comfort. I had started back trying to work out but it's hard to work out with Nolan. Most of the time when I get off work and pick him up it's already almost three or four something in the afternoon, I usually have to go to the grocery store, pick up food, or cook which is time consuming. Clean the house, keep an eye on Nolan, make sure he isn't getting into stuff, work on my business plan for my business, it's just a lot. The everyday routine of my life has become so busy that exercising now falls to the bottom of my list of things to do. And a social life, what the hell is that anymore. Being a mom and working has literally become my life. So maybe I was too much of a bore compared to before. I don't know. Even the me I am now I am still getting used to. Then still trying to wrap my head around everything still has me a little baffled but I am working to move on.

It is just so many questions I had initially. Like, why not just take a walk around the block and blow off some steam opposed to leaving all together?

Maybe I was wrong but I don't see where the argument was that bad for him to give me such a cold shoulder. When exposing my truth, I never once said we could never be together again, I just said I needed time to heal still. Because to recommit to him with some much distrust already in my heart was disloyal. I could see myself loving him again, but sex was not going to heal my heart and mind. That was going to take time. It seems hypocritical but the throbbing between your legs can sometimes feel louder than the beating of your heart and thoughts. And sexually I was attracted to him still and still had love for him, but to just throw caution to the wind and be back in love with him was something I knew I was not ready for. To even enter into a relationship again would have been unfair. I don't know, some days as I am watching one of my evening shows on BET, the tv will be more so watching me as I space out from my thoughts, playing the day over and over in my head of how things could have gone differently. Maybe I should have just given in. I feel like I was fighting so hard to stand up for myself. I finally had instead of just feeling like he was walking all over me, and now I am alone and feel unwanted.

Then my not supporting him wanting to sell pills and get back in the streets is also no reason to not talk to me. I get it would have been for a short period of time, but I know that sometimes the streets are like a gang. Sometimes they don't let you out just because you want out. It becomes almost like an addiction, I've seen it too much. Then there was the jeopardizing of my child and my safety as well as my career. Plus I couldn't understand for the life of me why he was going backwards. When we were together he was on the straight and narrow. Once he went back to Ginger, all that shit hit the fan. He came back with this mindset that the streets were a place of loyalty and could be trusted. When in fact the game is not loyal to anybody, some shit can go wrong at any given moment and quickly. I still loved him effortlessly and was willing to fight for him to rebuild. So how could he not see that I had his back. Had I not shown that already. I try not to linger on it, but it's hard to not try to piece together the puzzle of how a man you made a child with, loved you so he said, and you loved him all of a sudden turns into a living ghost.

I am far from perfect but the love I had to give him, I was more than willing to give. In that short amount of time, being around Keiontay was like me relapsing. The wounds I thought I closed were reopened and I realized that I never healed them but just put a bandaid on them. However, this time it seemed a lot more like I was going to have to go cold turkey again, but this time my supplier of my drug was gone, and this time almost felt worse than the first. After about three months of not hearing anything from him, I thought about reaching out to his mother. Yet I decided against it as my plate was running over like a gallon of water in a sippy cup. I was back working full time, Nolan was going to daycare, and my mom was out in the wind trying to find a purpose for herself. I respected that but I needed help. I truly hated my baby having to be in daycare, but I had to do what I had to do to provide for us. I thought I would have Keiontay, my mom, or somebody to help me, but I could not have been more wrong. Mentally I felt like I was being pulled in a hundred and one directions. I now had adopted so many hats that I felt like I was weighing myself down, but it felt wrong to complain.

The world we live in says that if you get what you want you can't complain about it, just do it and be happy. To complain says you're ungrateful and don't want what you asked for, but for me it says you are human. That even in what you want, working to keep it can be overwhelming and that was me. I carried no regret and loved every blessing in my life but the human side of me was overwhelmed. So as I worked and mom'd, I shut out the world and dealt with my pain alone. Nobody reached out to me, and I was tired of reaching out to people. I needed somebody to reach out for me, check on Nova, check on Nolan, but nothing. So many days I came home and just cried as my son uttered his first words of DaDa, but there was no DaDa, only me to even share in that moment. I wish I could have called Keiontay and shared it with him. Nolan's learning how to pull up on things, how to balance himself and learn how to walk, all these first I just cherished alone.

My mother facetimed him and shared in the moment that way, but his mother and father had no connection or even made an attempt to meet Nolan. No facetime, video chat, text or anything . It was as if, since Keiontay wasn't involved with me they didn't have to be involved with Nolan either, so I was definitely carrying a lot on my shoulders. I never wanted to continue a generational curse, break it if anything, especially when it comes to an upbringing. And already I was seeing the cycle about to repeat. Keiontay used to claim he never wanted to be like his father, in the streets so much it takes him from his child and boom he chooses the streets. My biological father walked out long ago, my step dad is addicted to gambling and cheating, and now boom the cycle continues because now my son is going to grow up without his father. And the worst part of why it hits me so deep is because it's like my life is replaying through the eyes of my son almost.

My biological father too was alive but decided not to be in my life. Aware of my existence but chose to live his life without even caring if I'm breathing or not. I guess the naive side of me thought that since Kaleigh wasn't his daughter and Nolan is his son that he would be more than happy to stick around and be a father. Most men live for the day they have a son, and here it was his first born son, and it still didn't matter. Was I standing in the way of my son having a father by not doing what he wanted when he asked? I felt like I was and even considered paying him to come around if money is what he was focused on, but then I realized it wouldn't be sincere if I did that. I would never want anyone to pretend to love me nor my son so I let that idea go. It was just too much. I was fighting a losing battle, and then to add fuel to the fire about a month after he first left I realized my period still was a no show. I had waited my six weeks, and Keiontay was the only person I slept with. In the short time he was here, when we did start having sex we went at it and like an idiot used not a condom to the first.

That month after he left my heart was beating out of my chest damn near as I was cleaning my bathroom one Saturday morning while Nolan sat in front of the tv with his bowl of cheerios and a glass of milk. My son for some reason didn't like certain cereals together, but anyway. As I reached under the counter for the mango Lysol toilet bowl cleaner, I noticed my green Always pads and realized I did not remember having my period for that month. I immediately dropped everything and ran to get my phone to check my period app to confirm. My period was supposed to come at almost the start of the month on the 3rd and it's a whole other month and the pads under the cabinet were still sealed. I immediately started panicking, went to grab my coat to throw over of my Fenty grey onesie, took Nolan out of his high chair, threw him on his Nike bubble coat, grabbed my wallet and keys, and headed out of the door to get a pregnancy test because I think the fuck not.

To repeat another pregnancy with the stress that came from being pregnant by Keiontay had me driving, praying, and talking to God on the way to the neighborhood Walmart that was about 10 minutes away from my apartment. I prayed I was overreacting because I thought the timing before wasn't good, but this time definitely wouldn't be good as I would be completely on my own for sure this time. And mentally I wasn't sure if I could handle that. As we made it to the Walmart, I parked and ran in with Nolan on my hip to the family planning section feeling a little embarrassed but fuck it, I needed to know for sure. I grabbed a 3 pack First Response test, headed to self check out and was back out the door. I figured it was best to go home and freak out in the comfort of my own home.

I made it home, put my son back in front of the tv, threw my stuff off and searched for the first cup I could find to pee in. I had some plastic shot cups left and that was right on time for this moment and to the bathroom I went. As I peed and dipped the tips of all three sticks in my cup of urine, I sat them down to wait, I began to pace the floor waiting for those three minutes felt like an entirety. I was replaying my life over in my head thinking how I should have kept my damn legs closed. But I convinced myself that even if it was positive, I would have my kid, do the best I could and handle my damn business. Because as a mother, that's what you do. You make shit work. So though I was nervous and scared shitless it was what it was. Hell, at least in my kids I would get me some consistent, everlasting love, but this time I just wouldn't tell Keiontay. Hell because what difference would it make for him to know. At least not helping with a child you don't know about is a different story and makes more sense, than one that you do know about, and don't help with.

As I stopped pacing, I just stood still and looked up at the ceiling and asked myself if I had been having any symptoms and just too busy to notice. As I shook my head at myself and then dropped it, I opened my eyes to see the results, and all three of them sent me to the floor on my ass with shock.

CHAPTER 3
Omar

It's an old saying that says, closed mouths don't get fed. When I was younger, I used to just think that meant asking for something, but now I know the meaning is deeper than that. It can mean a bunch of shit honestly, but another thing I took it to mean, is that if you don't ever open your mouth and speak up for what you want, you will never get it. And because I grew up in the hood, I hated that shit and a lot of my upbringing honestly made me bitter. I can admit that, but how to fix it, I never gave that another thought. My mother left when I was about five because she said it was too much for her, and my dad raised me but he was more in love with alcohol than the responsibility to be a parent to me. So these streets are where I found love. Not because I wanted to but because the streets gave me people that were more consistent than the people that helped create me. The older I got the angrier I got because shit didn't seem to get better, only worse it seemed like. I was raising myself while other kids had parents to love them, then I had a little brother and sister. So as the oldest they looked up to me. That was a lot of pressure. I loved my siblings, but I counted down the days until I graduated high school and got the fuck on.

I was tired of being strong for them, trying to keep everything together and was tired as hell on the inside, but as their protector, I made sure nobody ever hurt them, or they went hungry while our father constantly was more devoted to Jack Daniels, Tennessee Whiskey then he could ever be to us. When I was young, I figured he was using alcohol to mask the pain of my mother leaving, but after a while the shit just became a big excuse and everything left to fall on me. So my goal was to get the fuck out of the hood, make something out of myself, and make sure my siblings always knew they got me. Yeah I sold drugs here and there because it kept us fed and a roof over our head. Hell some days I even gave blood to make sure we ate. I did that and I love my siblings with everything in me, they are all the family I have and I would do it all again. But in the long run the shit fucked me up. Instead of it making me strong, it left a part of me bitter and closed off. Shit makes me walk around in this world like I don't give a fuck about nothing but thats not true.

Woman after woman, I never gave a fuck about them because I figured every woman I met reminded me of my mother and how heartless a woman could be. So yes, I was that player, the asshole, heartless ass pretty boy, whatever stereotype that is that applies to light skin dudes, I lived up to every one of them. To me that is what they deserved, and I saw nothing wrong with that. No, I was not going to commit, what was the point in somebody that would break my heart and leave me. I saw my dad turn into an alcoholic bitch over a woman he loved. Drank so much he damaged his liver. He could have moved on, but she fucked him up and I be damned if that ever be me. And the repercussions of the females that get mad and bust my windows, put sugar in my tank bull shit was dust on my shoulders. It was all replaceable just like they were to me.

Once I graduated from high school, I went to a trade school for hvac (heating, ventilation, and air condition) , got certified and was working odd and end jobs. That is how I managed to pull us out of the hood to something nice, and I vowed to myself to always make sure my family was straight and the money came first. At the age of 31, I still have the same motto I keep near and dear, so I let nothing in and nobody stands in the way of that. Pussy come and go, so that's a given. I honestly don't have to do much to get a female. Between being a dread head, light skinned, tatted, I dress nice, and you can tell I got a little bread, Hmph, it isn't hard to get a bitch pussy wet when they look at me. Panties will be dropped and off before I can get my name out good. I've made it to 31 with no kids, single, on my shit, and I can't stand alcohol. I love the man I am becoming, and for a while I thought nothing was wrong with me. I had it all in my book. Life content, no worries, and happiness.

From the outside looking in, I might come off as mean, but that anger stays hidden so I'm not mad at the world, just mad at how certain shit turned out for me. Life goes on. But there was one job I took on and the woman attached to it, fucked me up. All my roughness and I don't give a fuck about love and shit went out the window the minute I laid eyes on her. When I saw her, I for once felt something in my body that I had never felt for any woman, and the funny part was I didn't even know she existed. I was simply there because it was the middle of winter and her heat had gone out.

The apartment complex maintenance guy was out sick, and they called me in to handle the job, and when it comes to money, I go get it so there was no turning it down. In my line of work, I come across a lot of females that see me and want me the minute I walk in the room to fix something. They love the idea of me fixing shit and looking good while doing it. I slept with some, and others I just kept professional, but from the moment she came out on her balcony to help me find the right apartment because my gps was malfunctioning; I wasn't sure what she looked like but while looking for the apartment, I seen a woman that had me about to crash into a tree her beauty was so captivating. Once I noticed that the woman I was looking at was the woman on the phone giving me directions, I just knew I had to get her number somehow.

Once I parked and went in, I had an associate with me that peeped her too, but I refused to let anybody mess up this opportunity. I sent my associate back to the shop claiming I forgot one of the fuses, which I didn't need so I could work alone with this woman. As I worked she talked to me and I'm not sure what I was feeling, but she was different from every other woman I ever came across. How? Shit'd on plenty of levels. Hell, for one I couldn't even tell if she was truly into me, but I was just hoping she was. I saw she wasn't married, I didn't hear any kids so hopefully that meant no baby daddy drama, so I shot my shot before I left out of the door. For the first time in my life, I was nervous to ask a woman for her number, but as I headed to the door, I stopped and asked if I could call her sometimes.

She blushed and smiled, and her smile sent chills all over my body. Shit was crazy, and when she gave me her number, I felt like that day was the best day of my life. From the time I got back in my work truck I texted her in hopes it was the right number, and hoped to hear from her. Shawty had me with butterflies in my stomach. I figured maybe I was just getting old and the player in me was dying. When she replied and said she was locking in my number, I fist pumped the air with a smile on my face that scared me, it was so unfamiliar. I felt like I had my first crush. I saved her name as Nova, but had a blushing emoji by her name. Weird shit man. Idk what was going on with me, but once we agreed on a day to go on a date that fit both of our work schedules it all made sense, why I felt she was so special.

We agreed to meet at the restaurant because she was getting off later than usual because they had some late shipments of prescriptions to come in, and I understood because I still was re-wiring an office downtown before I could head home so that was perfect. I was excited. I wanted to stop and get her flowers, but time was close and I didn't want to be late. Since that morning before my first job of the day I had laid my clothes out like a kid's first day of school outfit. All I had to do was hop in the shower and get ready. I was dripping in Alexander McQueen from head to toe. From my black harness sport long sleeve button down shirt, embroidered black straight leg jeans, to make my black and white McQueen shoes to match, with my gold 10k Cuban link chain to top it off. I wanted to look good for her. We had agreed on Benihana's on Peachtree so that wasn't too far from her nor me, so we would hopefully be on time, and boy was I ever ready to see her.

I managed to get there before her, and when she arrived I was waiting outside of the building. When she was walking towards me in this green Armani slip dress and gold Tom Ford heels, hair blowing in the wind with a black London Fog pea coat on. Man, I wanted to take her down in the parking lot. When I met her she had on a school shirt from her college and some shorts, looked like she was just home chilling, and seeing her dressed up like this was a super turn on. She looked stunning.

As I took her hand and we headed inside the restaurant, we were seated, and everything was going so great. We shared a shrimp tempura roll for an appetizer, laughed and talked like we had known each other since way back. Shit was amazing. She had the teriyaki chicken, hibachi steak, fried rice, and a salad, and I had the hibachi supreme that included steak and lobster with rice and vegetables. I remember almost every part of our first date because it was so special to me honestly. When it came time for dessert, they had switched our waiter out and the waiter said, "sir your girlfriend is absolutely beautiful. You are a lucky man." I didn't correct him, she was beautiful but the thought of commitment was something that made the mood awkward for me because commitment was something I didn't do, but when it came to her it made me want to reconsider but run at the same time.

Shit was crazy and had my mind racing, but I put that thought off and I figured I was too afraid of old hurt to create something new and special. So I figured hey I could just enjoy the moment, but she had my mind fucked up. Before our date, we had been texting through the week here and there, and I had revealed to her that I was stepping out on faith and trying out to be a firefighter. One of my life long dreams that I never spoke of. And how I had passed my exams, and was cleared to go on to training. Something big to me, but just me sharing with her cause it was in the moment. After the date ended and I walked her to her car, she told me to come to the trunk of the car with her, and this woman shocked the fuck out of me. She considered it not much but it was more than she ever could have known for me. In the trunk, were three congratulatory balloons, and a card with a firefighter on the front, a message on the inside that said congratulations, you're climbing the ladder in life. Congrats on your new beginnings, sincerely Nova E. with a $25 Chick-Fil-A gift card tapped to the other side.

Man, when I tell you that shit blew my mind cause no woman had ever, I mean never done a thoughtful ass gesture as such. I damn near wanted to cry, but I hugged her instead cause for once in my life I was speechless and it was attached to a good reason of why I was. Everything about her screamed the one, but my childish hurt and parts of immaturity began to talk me out of what could be. Then in the midst of my doubt, I felt she was one that wouldn't walk away, and wouldn't want to so I hoped. That night before we departed she also told me to drive safely, and let her know when I was home, and again to have somebody care about me coming home outside of my brother and sister was something unfamiliar for me. Other females wanted me for what I looked like and the dick I gave them, her, she wanted me for me. And I hadn't even gave her the D. She was just ginuwine, but of course my insecurities and not fully ready to let go of my past I started to sabotage a good thing despite how I felt like a jack ass, and it led to me losing her damn near and I can't blame nobody but myself to fuck up a good thing because she was doing everything right. It was me that started hiding in the shadows, and left her out in the open.

CHAPTER 4

"Mr. Clark, we are going to release you to go home tomorrow, but in order to be released, someone will have to be here to sign for you. The medication we are going to send you home with, you will not be able to operate your vehicle on your own. Plus until you complete physical therapy, I highly suggest you to not drive, do any heavy lifting, or excessively attempt to walk until cleared," the nurse said as she came in to check Keiontay's vitals and share what the doctor had told her to disclose.

"Ma'am, I can take care of myself perfectly fine, What did y'all do with my car?" he asked as he sat in the bed to look at the female nurse talking to him.

"I can ask around Mr. Clark as I do not have much knowledge of you having a vehicle. Did you drive yourself here?"

Exhaling with frustration as he began to grow short with the nurse, "Yes, I drove myself here, but I don't remember much after passing out. I need my car to be able to drive home. I'm tired of being here."

"Mr. Clark, I completely understand your frustration, but I will ask about your car. However, like I mentioned, you are not able to drive yourself."

"So y'all are going to hold me hostage like a criminal because I got stabbed?" he said with anger.

"No sir, that is not what we are trying to do at all. We just want the best for you. Your safety matters. We would not want you to leave and have to come right back here, or worse come back without treatment as an option," she stated.

Keiontay said nothing as he turned his attention to the television that he could not hear, but recognized the Martin episode that was on. He found himself tuning out the nurse and fixated on the screen until she tapped him on the shoulder causing him to jump with fear.

"I didn't mean to startle you, but I wanted to be sure that you understood we needed to talk to the person that we will release you to, to confirm them agreeing to coming to get you. Also, we asked before, but I'm not sure if you remember, but if you want to press charges on the person that did this to you we can still have the police come in and make a report for you."

Shaking his head at the thought of having to call anyone that knew him was something he wished he could get around. and who did it to him was something even he wished he knew.

Completely avoiding her second statement about the police, "Okay, can you give me my phone?" he asked, feeling perplexed.

"Mr. Clark, you do not have to be afraid to report the person," she interjected as she stood there with concern in her eyes as she looked at him.

"I don't know who fucking did it! I was damn near blind and losing blood. I had no time to stop and take a picture with the motherfucker!" Keiontay said with anger in his voice.

"I don't want to upset you. I was just letting you know that if you had remembered by chance that we could help."

"I'm sure, can you just give me my phone so I can try and do what y'all are asking so I can get the hell on."

"I will give you the bag with your belongings in them, and I will let you get it out," the nurse explained as she turned to go get his bag off the little brown table stand under the television.

"If you need anything else Mr. Clark please do not hesitate to press the call button, and the doctor will be in to talk with you after she makes her rounds," she explained.

As the nurse turned to leave, Keiontay said, "wait," causing the nurse to stop and turn back to him to see what he wanted.

"Yes, sir, what can I do for you," she inquired.

"Look, I got $500 in my jeans that you can have if you get them to release me without me having to hear from anybody. I will just take the chance and drive myself or take a Lyft."

"First off, I cannot accept that Mr. Clark and secondly, I don't think you understand the severity of your situation. Maybe it wasn't explained well enough on my end, so when the doctor comes around I will let her go over your circumstances again. If by chance you want to call a Lyft driver and that's all of who you have to come then fine, but we still need to make sure that the driver could at least help you to get inside your residence."

Exhaling as he turned his attention back to the television, the nurse said nothing else as she noticed his annoyance and turned to leave.

As he sat there in bed feeling almost completely numb, he realized he had a hard time trying to move his leg. In his attempts to move his right leg, it felt heavy and it brought tears to his eyes.

"I ain't never did nothing so fucking bad to anybody to deserve this shit right now. What if I never walk right again?," he thought to himself as he held his phone lost in his thoughts. "Then I feel like I have nobody at this point. I'm not sure who to trust and what bridges I have burned."

He went to unlock his phone using face recognition and it was unable to read his face. He grew frustrated and opened the camera on the front screen to see why his phone was not recognizing him, and his right eye was swollen and some stitches were on his eyebrow. In the moment, he looked at himself and a tear rolled down out of his left eye.

"This is what I get for turning back to the streets. I had turned my life around. What the fuck? Who am I even at this point? I feel like I don't even know myself anymore. I just keep fucking up. I'm not a good father, an asshole to the woman I love, haven't talked to my folks, then I haven't even been taking care of myself. So consumed with the quick money and temporary love of the streets that I got blindsided and almost ate alive," he thought as he held his phone. Finally deciding to just use his passcode to unlock his phone, he tapped his contacts and shook his head. As he knew there was no one in his phone that he wanted to explain himself to, hear I told you so from, or was even sure he could trust.

"I come out better just taking a Lyft. That way I don't have to be bothered with any damn body. I refuse to call my mother and hear her mouth. There's a high chance Nova will come but to let her see she was right, hell no. Ginger..fuck no..I would rather let them keep me, Tarven pussy whipped ass...fuck no. Then there's Malachi, but I get the feeling that I might have seen him already without having to call for him. I have to get that man his money back so I can close that chapter of my life. I'm ready to take me back. No scratch that! I'm ready to be the man that I need to be. I owe that to Nolan and myself. I wouldn't blame Nova for not wanting me back. This time I will wait until things are better in me before entering back into their lives prematurely . It's not too late for me to save myself from myself," he continued thinking as he backed out of his contacts and opened the Lyft app.

As he opened the app, he checked to see what the price would be from the hospital to the hotel he had made home. This was something else he was disappointed in himself about. He long ago was supposed to get his own apartment, but with his attachment to the streets and fast money, he was struggling to let go. So when he had told Nova he would get a place after a period of time, all of that had been put on the back burner. But no longer. He was ready to redeem himself after going through this ordeal.

"From Piedmont Atlanta Hospital to Hawthorn Suites by Wyndham..." he started to say out loud as he entered the information.

Selecting to be picked up from the main entrance of the hospital, "$25 is not bad at all. A good price, I don't have to bother anybody, don't have to explain shit to anybody and I will be back in the comfort of my room, finally! I will just keep this screen up until they tell me it's time to put it in for pick up. Problem solved," he said smiling as he fluffed his pillow slightly and laid his head back feeling as though he dodged the headache of having to put anyone in his business.

Before he put down his phone, he went to his photos and saw the picture of Nolan when he first learned how to walk. It made him smile as he reflected on what it was like to be there to witness that moment.

"I have to get myself together. I already missed so much in the beginning from dealing with Ginger and now I'm missing the parts I could be a part of because of my own behavior. I can't blame anybody but myself at this point," he said as he shook his head. As a reminder, he used the picture of Nolan as his home screen and lockscreen for inspiration that though he's fallen, he too could get up and walk again and not just physically.

As he turned his phone off to conserve the 20% he had holding on, the doctor knocked on the door and entered the room.

"Mr. Clark," the doctor started to say to get Keiontay's attention.

Slightly turning over to face the doctor unprepared for what she had to say because the thought of hearing about his wounds was a reminder of the traumatic day he wished he could forget. As he said nothing, he just looked at the doctor to try and mentally prepare himself.

"I was coming around anyhow to check your bandages and stitches before your discharge, but the nurse informed me that you're not understanding the severity of your recovery once discharged. This is why assistance is needed upon us letting you go," she stated as she looked at him.

"I'm not stupid, I understand the severity but I honestly just don't have anyone I trust right now to help me. I trust myself so I'll do the best I can," he stated firmly.

"Mr. Clark, I'm sure you have someone but you're being stubborn in reaching out to them, and right now pride should not be at the forefront. You're lucky that you're honestly still here with the amount of blood you lost. From your stomach to your hip. We were able to prevent infection from spreading in your stomach due to the stabbed wound. The antibiotics are sterilizing and fighting off any lingering bacteria as well as for your hip. Whoever stabbed you definitely was not playing fair using an old and dirty knife. But between your stitches and bandages needing to be changed either we can send someone home with you, or you can assure us that someone will be helping you."

Keiontay said nothing and let the doctor continue to talk. “I get you’re strong and could take care of yourself but now is not a time to be alone.”

Finally breaking his silence, “ok, ok, I hear you. I get it. Somebody will help me. No need to send me any home help aids.”

“Well if by chance the person you’re thinking about doesn’t work out, you can call back and we will get someone scheduled to come out for you. My job is to not just care when you’re in my presence but once you leave as well. I don’t want you to have to come back unless it’s for something good.”

“I hear you. So when are you discharging me so I can schedule my ride?” Keiontay asked.

“Well, based on your chart your pain tolerance is good, blood pressure is down, and there is no sign of infection so in about an hour or two. I will get your medications written up, instructions for follow up care, recommended doctors and contacts, give you a small dosage of morphine, and then I can send you on your way,” she explained as she closed his chart and turned to leave the room with nothing else to say.

Keiontay took out his phone and thought about reaching out to Nova so that he wouldn’t be alone, but then a part of him felt he deserved to be. “I got myself into this mess thinking quick money was the way to go and got greedy. It’s not fair to add her to more of my mess. After all, I've put her through enough. Hell, I got her raising our child by herself. There's no telling what all she's sacrificing, missing out on, etc to make sure our son is straight. I feel like a fool for sure. I know if I tell them that a part of me feel like I don't care if I live or die at this moment with so much I've fucked up, they're liking to not release me. I don't want to kill myself but if I die, I feel like oh well it's just my time," Keiontay thought to his self as he powered his phone back on and it vibrated almost instantly with a notification.

@WinningSmileG wants to send you a message, the Instagram notification said.

With him changing his number and blocking most of the problems he was running away from, little to no one had access to him. So he was curious to who it was but with the G at the end of the username, he had a good feeling of who it could be. He certainly was in no mood to deal with her bullshit, but his curiosity got the best of him to know at least what it said.

@WinningSmileG: Hey, I know I'm the last person you probably want to talk to, but I'm truly sorry. I shouldn't have hurt you like that, but I didn't know how to let go of my hurt without feeling like I had to pay you back and that was wrong of me. I know better but my hurt blinded me. I hope maybe in time we can sit down and talk. At least become associates again. I miss you and the thought of not having you in my life at all makes me miserable. Which is why I wanted to hold on to the lie for so long. I knew the minute you found out there was a chance I could lose you forever. Again, I'm sorry and please reach out if this message finds you.

Deleting the message and then exiting the app, he shook his head as the nurse came in with his final shot and discharge papers. "You can go ahead and call your ride. About time they get here, the medication should have kicked in, I can check your blood pressure one last time, and then we can wheel you down, and you'll be good to go," she said.

"Thank you and my apologies earlier for seeming as though I was giving you a hard time," he said as he looked at the nurse and realized she was attractive. A new woman in his life was the last thing he needed so he quickly let the thought leave his mind.

"I forgive you, but it's only because you're kind of handsome. Otherwise, yes you were quite rude," she stated as she began to smile.

As she gave him the morphine dosage in his IV, she placed the discharge papers on his bed and then started to go over them with her copy. When finished she asked for his signature to confirm that he understood everything and that she did go over the packet.

"Such a bold signature, you must sign a lot of paperwork or do something pretty amazing with a signature like that," she complimented.

"I thank you for the compliment but I actually don't. I can boldly admit that I'm in the process of trying to create a better me. My mistakes have run enough of the course," he stated.

"Well I certainly understand that, if you ever need somebody to talk to, I put my name and number on the back of the last page of your discharge papers. I hope to hear from you," she said and smiled as she looked him in his eyes.

"What's your name?" He asked.

"Morgan," she said as she continued to look him in his eyes.

"Beautiful name to match a beautiful person," he said, returning a compliment.

" I can't lie, the me a couple of days ago would have been typing your number in my phone, but I have to be honest and admit that I think I should just chill on dating right now."

"Dating? Who said anything about dating? I can just be a friend and truly just look out for you cause you and I both know you're not going to let anyone help you. You're too proud to ask for help, and feel whatever you did outweighs the fact that you're still human. No matter our mistakes we don't stop being human. It's just about us learning to forgive ourselves first and foremost, and then associating with those that respect that we are imperfect and have some healing to do," she stated.

"That's deep and I feel that. I respect you for sharing that with me. I needed to hear that," he stated as his body felt light as the medicine had finally kicked in.

"Well, I've done all I've needed to do. In about 30 minutes I'll be back to check your blood pressure and with a wheelchair to wheel you down to discharge," she stated and turned to leave.

As she left the room, he picked up his phone and scheduled for a Lyft to pick him up in forty five minutes just to be safe. He didn't want the driver to drive off so he figured those 15 minutes would spare him. And like clock work, he was dressed in some scrubs that the hospital gave him since his clothes were basically destroyed, and the nurse was back in 30 minutes like she said she would. It was like the perfect timing as he got notified that his driver was arriving. As she handed him his belongings bag and discharge papers, they headed out of the room to the elevators to head downstairs.

"I'm starting to think you like me a little or either you're really bored. Don't they usually have someone else to do this," Keiontay said, trying to make small talk.

"You're cute, but yes we do, but he is on his lunch break so I was just helping out. We could go back in your room to wait on him," she joked as they got onto the elevator and shared a laugh. "Ah dang!" she blurted out.

"What, what's wrong?"

"I just feel like you smiled and I missed it."

Slightly laughing again, "I must have been a pretty bad patient," he said as the elevator doors opened.

"Only when you were awake were you most annoying," she said and started laughing.

"You sure, you're not a comedian instead of a nurse," he said, starting to laugh.

"Ha ha ha, you're funny, now what kind of vehicle should we be looking for before I leave you here," she said with a chuckle.

Forgetting to check before leaving the room, he pulled out his phone, unlocked it, opened the app to see what type of car to look for and the driver's name, and he started to think that his luck could not be that damn bad.

"You gotta be kidding me! Please let there be another motherfucker in this world that looks exactly like him," he thought to himself.

"What's wrong," she asked, noticing him shift in the chair and exhale as though he saw something he didn't like.

"I don't want to talk about it, I'm about to cancel this Lyft. I'm not sure if you have to wait with me, but you don't have to. I just don't have time for this right now."

"Is the driver already here?" she inquired.

"It says he has arrived, but I know the driver and I don't think he should be taking me anywhere."

"If you have a problem with the person and do not trust them, it is best you cancel and call for another driver, as you are not in any predicament for any new problems."

"My point exactly," he started to say as he unlocked his phone, opened the app, and canceled the ride, but preventing the drama he wanted to avoid was too late.

CHAPTER 5
Tarven

The only thing I wanted was to freely be able to love the woman that I loved, and that woman for me was Ginger. I loved everything about her and felt like life without her didn't make sense. I needed her to be a part of my life by any means necessary. So whatever she wanted for me to do, I did. Now sometimes I rebel because Ginger is the type that if you let her get an inch, she will take off and do damn 5 miles. There were times I had to put my foot down, and remind her who the man was in the relationship. I regret the days of putting my hands on her, but I didn't know how to express my emotions which was wrong. I was getting sick and tired of the games she had me playing to appease her when it came to this crazy ass love triangle that I never wanted.

She suggested I dated other women to not make it obvious that she and I were together, I did it. She asked me to move in with Keiontay to be her extra set of eyes, I did it. She wanted the details on Nova once that relationship got started, so I did it. She knew how deep my love was and took advantage of that and I hated that shit. I wanted her too bad to walk away. Then there was my., I don't even want to say jealousy because that's not the word, but maybe a little envious when it came to Keiontay. A part of me truly saw him like a brother to me, but him always being chosen first was something that played on my mind every time. From the time we were kids, everybody always flocked to be on Keiontay's team, wanted to hang with him, go to his house, whatever. It sounds juvenile, but I was there for him. I was the big brother he always wanted. Yeah, he looked out for me when I needed him, put me on to joints, but I just didn't feel he truly valued me as a friend. So a part of me got mad, and my envy led me to wanting him to feel as small as me for all the times he did it to me.

I don't care if he didn't know, that didn't stop the fact that it bothered the hell out of me. Then having to pretend to not know about my first born was something else that ate me up inside. However, that was a little worth it to know that when he found out he would feel the emptiness I felt when it comes to feeling overlooked. I hated not being there to see my baby girl being born, but in order to stick to the plan, I had to play my role, no matter how bad it hurt. My baby girl being born actually changed my life and softened my heart. I started regretting my choices, but my love for Ginger still had me torn. I started to get territorial because Ginger and Kaleigh are my family, my blood, and risking spending time with them because of some old shit that I couldn't control all started to sound quite foolish. I had to keep it real with myself. The problem was me and my insecurities. I was discrediting myself and not seeing the worth in myself. I was working so hard to be in his shadow that I didn't realize being myself had its own rewards.

Ginger wanted me originally, but when she saw Keiontay, I assumed what was going to happen because of past situations. So I pushed her away, pretended like I didn't want her and didn't care who she dated. I've been mad at myself for all these years, and it took Kaleigh being born for me to realize that. Now, I can't lie when I first saw Nova, I was like damn and thought about trying to make a move on shawty but knowing the daughter he loved was truly mine was enough. Plus she seemed like she only had eyes for him and you could see that shit a mile away. Ginger's hate and obsession for Nova was solely all her. The minute I mentioned that she was there the day I went over, she started searching, snooping, and plotting. Which is crazy because I feel like in a sick sense that is why Ginger and I do mash well because we have the same crazy ass mind. Not the best thing to have in common, but hey that's just us. We love strong and sometimes wrong.

Yeah, I was getting tired of the games I was playing. About to be 32 in a few months with a kid, and a woman. It was time to stop being childish which is why I was going to tell Keiontay myself that day about Kaleigh and everything. To not hurt him was too late because the damage was already done. I knew the part of me that valued our friendship was definitely going out the door when shit hit the fan, but Ginger beat me to it and left me with my back against the wall. Yes, I finally would be able to be with the woman I loved and spend more time with my daughter, but to lose my friend ended up hurting me more than I thought it would. Made me feel disappointed in myself because was all of what I did even worth it, I questioned some days.

They say be careful what you ask for and sometimes what you think you want isn't always what you need. Now I understand the days when Keiontay and I used to talk and he was telling me how she was getting on his nerves. Of course we were messing around at that time too but we weren't living together. The truth of truly learning somebody is when you live with them is the got damn truth. I kept my apartment, but moved most of my stuff in with her since she had the most room at her place, and for the first half of the transition shit was weird. I damn near slept on the sofa for about two weeks before moving fully into the bedroom with her. Just odd stuff, but I still love her, don't get me wrong, but now that it's just us, I didn't realize she was so much work, and requires so much attention. I guess there was excitement in the chase and drama of it all. Now, I find myself sometimes running from the responsibility.

Ginger has been going through this depression phase that is mentally draining the hell out of me. While she's stuck in her feelings

I'm on Daddy duty. Kaleigh is walking, getting into stuff, learning how to talk, hell I have even started her on potty training. All me, while Ginger just goes to work and then comes back home and gets back in bed.

We have sex every once in a while. I think over the course of the year that has passed since everything went down we've had sex about 10 times. Maybe 12 if I think really hard, but overall the spice has been almost nonexistent. The sad part is I finally got what I wanted but at the same time, feel like I've lost so much. I love being a Dad, it's pretty cool to see the life you helped to create grow before your eyes. Every day I can see so many of my features and ways in her, and I love that. So when Ginger is bitchy, my little princess is the light in a dim day. I've tried to think of almost everything to bring her out of this mood, but I'm not sure if there is even a solution. Well one that doesn't include me losing her again. It was like stalking Nova and running behind Keiontay were the biggest parts of her life, and Kaleigh and I were second best.

Depressed Ginger is not one I am used to at all. I literally took on driving for Lyft to get out the house some. With a flexible schedule, I can literally work almost all damn day if I want to, which has been helping my pockets and my mind. I've been able to help Ginger more, was able to trade my old 2000 Toyota Camry out for a new 2019 all black Toyota Camry, splurge on my baby girl, and I'm saving for the perfect ring for Ginger. Maybe not perfect, but it's going to look damn good and show a great representation of my love for her. I just want her to realize what's in front of her, we're not going anywhere, and that we love her more than she knows. When she's ready I want her to know that I might get annoyed in why she's feeling how she does, but I love the fuck out of her, and will not leave her side. My goal is to be the best husband and father that I can be.

However, the saddest truth is that she misses Keiontay and hell I do too. I can't say what she misses about him cause I'm not in her body, but I miss my friend. Despite the way I might have felt, I know this man always had my back, and we could laugh about the craziest shit. He was like the little brother I always wanted. We had our own little code, and everything. Shit used to piss some people off but that's just something we created solely for us. Hell, the brother I have, he and I aren't close. With us having two different dads he took more to that side of the family and lives with his dad. We only see each other on holidays, some birthdays, and special occasions here and there, like his graduation or some shit. I couldn't even tell you if my little brother knows how to drive and if he does what type of car he has or even if he has one. I barely know anything about him, which is another reason Keiontay and I were so close. He understood me. I tried reaching out to him about two months after everything, and he had changed his number and blocked me on everything. It was understandable, if I was him, I wouldn't talk to me, but I need a chance to at least explain myself and apologize. The shit weighs on my consciousness. It was never a competition between us, only the one that I created in my head, which was a false reality that I started to believe.

If I ever get the chance to run into him, somehow....as a man, I want to right my wrongs as best as possible. I at least owe him that, I should have just let things play out and unfold how they were going to, but I had to put my hands in things.

With months into doing Lyft, picking up and dropping off customers had become second nature. Once Ginger left for work in the morning, I would drop Kaleigh off at daycare and then start my day. That had become my daily routine, and that was cool. I had become a family man, out of the street life, my player ways thrown away, and my customers added that excitement to my days. It was a great little mix. As the months went on, I started to just focus on getting my family stable physically, mentally, and emotionally. My daughter was doing good, but trying to shake Ginger out of her depression was a struggle. Any time I brought up her going to get help she always got defensive and said she's okay, and that she was just going with the motions of life. She said that maybe I was overreacting because nobody at work assumed she was sad or depressed. And I tell her every time that is because when she steps into those doors, she puts on a fake smile that says to the world she is okay when in all truth she wasn't.

I can tell her she needs help all day, and even lead her to it, but it is going to take her admitting and realizing that she does. I just hope that she can come out of this because I don't want to lose her. People do not understand how severe depression can be. I have been there, the voices in your head start to tell you shit and it isn't always easy to ignore them, but coming through it is the best part. Maybe I still need to step up my game. Maybe it's something I am doing wrong as a man that she needs and I'm missing. I'm no mind reader, but I'm trying.

Anyway, most of my customers are complete strangers. It is very rare that I have ever picked up anyone that I have ever met. So most of the time I don't pay much attention to the names of the people I pick up. When I arrive, I verify it's them and that's that, I don't think much else about it really. It is like an in and out type of job, I listen to my music and mind my business. Majority of the time, I can be in the middle of a ride, and they will add someone to my queue. That is more money for me unless I'm heading home, or have to go check on Kaleigh. This particular day I was going to call it short after my last ride because I wasn't feeling good.

I had eaten some microwave burritos I got from the dollar store for my so-called breakfast, and it had finally decided to catch up with me. As I dropped my last customer off at an aesthetic center, the system had already added another rider to my queue. I told myself hell naw not today. I pulled over to cancel the ride and was about to head home, but my eyes bucked when I saw Keiontay's name. The pick up location was at the hospital. Before jumping to conclusions, I tapped the profile picture and it was for sure him. What was he doing at the hospital? Why did he need a Lyft? Doesn't he have a car? Maybe I should just cancel it, but I've been waiting for an opportunity to apologize so maybe this is it...so instead of declining I proceeded to the route to pick him up. Plus his drop off location was only about 30 minutes from my place so if my stomach couldn't hold out, I could just run in and handle my business, and then head home.

The chance of a friendship was low but at least for my own conscience, my apology could finally be given. I've learned that sometimes apologies are more so for self than the person, and I was okay with that. I damn near floored it off the side of the road. Damn near almost hit somebody trying to take off. Glad I didn't but I was anxious because he had to clearly want to talk too since it shows my picture too. As the traffic lights seemed to be in my favor with each one of them turning green, I was almost there. I parked and hit arrived on my screen. I was looking in the rear view mirror like a crazy man trying to see if I saw him and hoped I would be able to recognize him.

As a minute rolled by, I noticed some one came out in a wheelchair that looked like him, but I wasn't sure. I wasn't going anywhere no matter how long it took him to come out. I know the wait time is five minutes, but he was the last rider for today and right now the rules didn't matter. However, my screen caught my attention as I noticed the ride had been canceled, but this was one rider I was not driving off from.

CHAPTER 6

Tarven took his keys out of the ignition, and got out of the car and prepared to head over towards Keiontay and the nurse that was standing next to him.

"Yo!" Tarven said as he approached Keiontay, grabbing his attention.

"Man, I don't have time for no bullshit! I just want to get home. See if y'all had let me drive myself I could have avoided this shit. There's no telling what this man got up his sleeve with the amount of hate he has in his heart for me."

"Mr. Clark, you are in no condition to drive and you know that. I am not leaving your side until I know you are in safe hands to get you home to lay down. If I need to call security to stand with us I will," Morgan interjected.

"Naw, security isn't needed. I know him and will take him home or where he needs to go," Tarven explained.

"Naw, I'm good! I'll call for another driver or switch over to another riding service," Keiontay rejected.

"It's been a year and I have tried calling and reaching out to you but you changed your number and blocked me. Bro, you got me standing here sounding like a bitch trying to explain and apologize," Tarven said.

"Cool, I hear you. I just want to get home, because the thought of looking at you makes me wish I could get out this chair and show you how I feel to see you right now and I promise you, it ain't a hug," Keiontay said as he looked Tarven up and down.

"And I deserve that but please hear me out. Let me take you home. I promise no matter how you feel about me, I still want you straight. Hell even if I just take you home and say nothing the whole ride. Let me do it, I owe you that," Tarven offered. "I will even give the nurse my phone number to ensure you will get home with no problems," he continued.

"Why, so Ginger will know where I am? I shouldn't even be surprised to see you with her crazy ass reaching out to me," Keiontay said as he unlocked his phone to download some more ride share apps as Tarven continued to stand there.

"She reached out to you?" Tarven asked as his eyes widened.

"I'm not doing this! What don't you understand! Whatever fucking games y'all trying to play, I dont't want to play. I promise staying away from the both of yall is more so for y'all safety and because I have a fucking heart for Kaleigh no matter how no fucking good and trifling her parents are. She didn't ask to be born to two fucked up individuals, so its best I keep my distance," Keiontay said as he waited for his app to download.

"Fuck it I can't make you let me take you home, but I will say my peace because you deserve it and I need to clear my conscious," Tarven stated.

"You about to say my fucking business in front of a stranger bro? Now you're trying to further embarrass me?" Keiontay asked, taking his attention from his phone.

"No, I just," Tarven started to say.

"Naw, I ain't no bitch! Let's go! However the dice roll my boy, shall they may cause I literally was being polite and asking you to leave me the fuck alone! Plus it's free! Let's go! Roll me on then my boy," Keiontay said as he looked at Tarven.

"Mr. Clark, are you sure? I don't mind continuing to wait with you for another ride" Morgan said.

"I'm a grown ass man, I can handle myself beautiful. I thank you though. No disrespect at all to you, but bruh said he was going to take me home. This is what happens when you run from certain shit, it has a bad habit of catching up to you!" Keiontay said.

"That is true, but I just want you okay," Morgan expressed with sincerity.

"And I appreciate that! I'll let you know when I get home," Keiontay said as he looked up at Morgan who had much concern in her eyes for him.

"Please, and if you don't I will be calling you, after all there's a whole chart on you," she said as she smiled slightly. "I'll wheel him to the car and we both can help get him in the car, and then you can take it from there," she said as she unlocked the brakes on the wheelchair and started pushing it towards Tarven's car as he led the way.

"Lord please let me make it home safely," Keiontay thought to himself as he started to get in the passenger seat of Tarven's car.

"Let me slide the seat back so you can be comfortable," Tarven said as he pressed the button on the side of the passenger seat for it to go back so he could have more room. "Do you want the seat back some more?" Tarven asked.

"Naw, I need to be sure of where I am going," Keiontay responded.

"Please be careful and make sure he gets home safely," Morgan said to Tarven as she shut Keiontay's door.

"I promise! Do you want my number to confirm when I drop him off?" Tarven asked.

"Oh no, I peeped your tag number," Morgan said as she winked at Tarven and walked off.

Walking around to the other side of the car to get in on the driver's side, Tarven got in and started the car. "Since you canceled the ride, I no longer have the address of where to take you. You will have to give me the address or give me some directions," he said as he tapped his phone to pull up the map prepared to put in an address.

"I'll tell you where to go, just drive," Keiontay said, feeling annoyed with his current circumstances.

"Man, this is Atlanta! I need to know where we going before we end up in Tennessee got damn," Tarven responded.

Continuing to look out of the window, Keiontay nodded his head in agreement. "You right plus I am ready to lay in the bed and not be disturbed by anybody. The hotel down near Hammond Dr.," he said vaguely.

"I guess when we get to Hammond Drive, you will give me further directions?" Tarven asked but Keiontay said nothing.

Not waiting for Keiontay to respond, Tarven started to drive and turned up the radio to drown out the awkward silence that filled the car. With an estimated 35 to 40 minute drive because an accident was on the route ahead, they had a good distance to go.

"How in the hell of all people did I get one of my enemies as a driver out of all the damn drivers in Atlanta? Like my luck has to be shitty," Keiontay thought to himself as he stared out of the window. "The days I spent waking up in the hospital were definitely eye opening for me, and I'm going to get my life together. But how does Tarven resurfacing in my life a part of me getting my life together? I guess, though I may not understand, even he has a purpose. I sure as hell don't need any new enemies on my radar, I already have to figure out who laid hands on me, and get Malachi his money back before shit with him goes completely left field and I end up dead for real," he continued to think.

Turning down the radio, Tarven broke the silence in the car as traffic came to a point of a stand still.

"Things got out of hand man, and with all my heart I truly apologize," Tarven said.

Laughing slightly, "You're saying things got out of hand like a fire in an abandoned building broke out from playing with one too many matches or too many people were in a venue and a fight emerged...things you could have no control over. The role and decisions you made that affected my life were something that you had control over and chose to do. I dead ass trusted you and saw you as my bro. There's no telling how many times you were stabbing me in the back, but I was steadily defending you and being there for you."

"You right, I did have the choice to choose better but I was blinded by love," Tarven started to say before Keiontay cut him off.

"Man gone with that lovey dovey bullshit cause I am not trying to hear that at all. Love doesn't mean deception," Keiontay said.

"And you're one to talk," Tarven interjected.

Looking at Tarven as they inched their way through traffic, "Fuck yeah, I am one to talk because none of the people that I hurt was ever intentional!" Keiontay said.

"It might not have been intentional but it still hurt them just the same," Tarven responded.

"See that's the problem with this world, steadily dancing into other people shit but not focusing on their damn selves. What you did has nothing to do with anybody else! As a man, my home boy, my brother, you could've come to me and said how you felt but you chose not to. Yeah, love can have you doing some stupid shit, but you became an enemy right under my nose and I never knew. Hell, I don't even trust that you won't tell Ginger about this and she won't pop up trying to start shit."

Scratching his head as Keiontay's words sunk in, "You right," Tarven managed to say.

"I've passed you bitches, we've shared bitches, but you couldn't tell me hey man I'm feeling shawty," Keiontay expressed.

"I did but your ego was too fucking big! I tried at some points but I saw she was more so into you then me. Well I thought she was, I got mad, and brushed shit off like it didn't bother me but it did. The way how people always have taken to you made me angry. A little envious and I wanted to bruise your ego," Tarven confessed.

"So you've been mad at me for some shit I can't control? How people treat me or take to me has nothing to do with me. I just be me and how people receive that has nothing to do with me. Coming up, I never force anybody to be my friend, hang around me or nothing. As an only child, I've been used to being alone. Hell I never even got attached to people because I never knew when they would leave, but not when it came to you. I trusted you, you were my brother, and you humiliated me," Keiontay said.

"I was, yes, but now since being a Dad, I see and understand my mistakes," Tarven started to say until he noticed Keiontay wiping his face. "I'm sorry for real."

"Man, I loved that little girl with everything in me. I fought to protect her, was scared to leave her around Ginger because of the shit she used to do to her. I literally watched her come out, there when she first said DaDa, and y'all took that from me. Do you know what it feels like to have to grieve somebody that is alive? Like I have no part in her life anymore. I thought I was somebody to her, a protector, a Father, but I was and am nothing to her. Shit got my head so fucked up that I have a biological child so I hope, that I haven't spoke to in a year because of you and Ginger's bullshit. I know Nova has my back more than anybody probably, but the days I saw my son, I wanted to ask her for a DNA test just to talk the devil down off my shoulder from telling me that she was lying. To fight the voice that maybe I don't deserve to be a Father! All this shit now flows freely in my head constantly! Do you know what the fuck that's like T? No, you don't because in y'all little plan you came out on top just how you wanted."

"You right, no, I don't, and I know sorry won't fix it, but I can't say it enough. It was actually Kaleigh and looking after her that helped me to see my mistakes. Made me want to do better and give you the apology you deserve. You honestly did not deserve the bullshit we put you through, and I wouldn't dare tell Ginger I saw you. Because I know in my heart I truly didn't win. Yes, maybe with no longer having to lie and missing out on my kid, but Ginger is no walk in the park and I know she still loves you. And if it means anything, in the time that you thought you were Kaleigh's Dad, you were doing good," Tarven said as he noticed that traffic was now moving along and they would be to Keiontay's destination soon.

Shaking his head, "Whatever bullshit Ginger dishes out to you always remember that you wanted it. And I 'ppreciate the apology but that's a tough wound to mend for me," Keiontay said. "I can't blame somebody else for how I'm handling things, but this definitely is a setback for me. I vowed to myself each day that I woke up in that hospital bed, that I would do better and make better decisions. So I can't say I forgive you, but I thank you for being man enough to apologize," he continued as Tarven came to the traffic light.

"Ppreciate it for real man, but where to? Do I keep straight or turn?" he asked Keiontay.

"Turn, it's going to be the hotel on the left side, the one that has suites in the name," he responded.

"Are you visiting somebody?" Tarven asked, trying to figure out what Keiontay had going on.

"If you can drop me off on the back, I'll make it the rest of the way," Keiontay said.

"Naw man, I don't care what way you might feel towards me and I know what was done was foul, but I'm not about to let you fall or no shit. At least let me get you to the door and whoever can take it from there," he said as he parked in front of the back door of the hotel.

Throwing his head back into the headrest feeling frustrated, Keiontay said, "fine! I will take that right about now cause that medicine got my head spinning."

Putting the car in park and getting out to help Keiontay, he grabbed his belongings, and put Keiontay's right arm around his shoulder. They walked at a snail's pace as they made it inside to the elevator.

Before Tarven could press the button of the elevator, Keiontay was out of breath and had to rest against the wall.

"You need to sit down on the floor man? You're sweating like hell!" Tarven said.

"No, I just want to make it to my bed and lay down," Keiontay said.

As Tarven pressed for the elevator to come down, Keiontay asked him if he could press the button for the 3rd floor. Tarven did as asked and as the elevator doors opened, Keiontay looked like he was about to pass out

"Man, do you want me to carry you? Like no funny shit. I can cause you sweating some serious and it's not even that hot," Tarven suggested.

"It's room 327, it's not that far down. I'm almost there," Keiontay said as he continued to use Tarven's shoulder for support.

"Man, you living here?" Tarven asked to squash his curiosity.

"This is me," Keiontay said as they made it to the door and used the key card to open the door. As Tarven opened the door and helped Keiontay into the bed, looking around Tarven answered his own question.

Keiontay laid back on the bed with exhaustion and wiped the sweat from his face.

"Man, what do you have going on? I've never known you to be living out of a hotel. Did shit get that bad for you?" Tarven asked as he continued looking around.

Continuing to lay back on the bed, Keiontay stared up at the ceiling, "shit didn't get bad, just the decision I made cause I wasn't sure whether I should stay or leave. No point in getting a place and I was going to be alone in it. So I didn't see much purpose in staying and still don't. Probably once I get full strength in my leg, I'm out," he explained.

"What about Nova and your son?" Tarven asked.

"The kid is probably better off without me. Nova is a good woman and a good mother, so I know she will raise him well," Keiontay said.

"But man, since we were little, we talked about if we ever had kids that we would never be the dads that ours was. That shit made us broken men, and here we are still learning as we're grown," Tarven said as he pulled out the chair that was under the desk by the window.

"Facts, but things change! Plus in my case, I basically became my dad already so why not see it out. Only difference is, I just didn't end up in jail, but I damn near ended up in a casket.

CHAPTER 7

Nova

Sometimes you do not think about the consequences of how things could turn out until you are placed in the crossfire of the flames.

Luckily, oh so graciously, all three tests read not pregnant. As I sat on the floor, I cried and talked to God because I was nowhere near ready for another child. I was bullshitting myself at the thought that I would be okay with it when I definitely wouldn't be. When I wiped my tears, I got angry. I don't know why but I was furious at myself and wished I could kick my own ass because it needed to be kicked. I felt like the woman I was working so hard to be had got deleted and a new version was installed that I was nowhere near prepared for.

On another note..... tired of my pity party of emotions and ruling out pregnancy, I decided to just get my life together. Wherever

Keiontay was he was focusing on him, so it was time to move on, and that's what I did. It's sad when I heard more from Omar asking how Nolan and I were than Keiontay, and it's not even Omar's son.

Over the course of the year, I worked and stayed to myself. No hook ups, no traveling, just my kid and I. Shit got lonely after about 8 months of feeling isolated. Omar called and texted periodically, but I just stopped answering calls and texts because I had gotten into a headspace where everybody was against me. Then around 10 months, it was the same thing, but my mom started reaching out. She had been MIA since she had last gone to a beauty conference, started working, making her own money, and had got her own place. Well at least that's what she told me. If she had a place, she usually would have invited us over by now, but nope. Outside of facetime calls, that's the only time Nolan and I saw her. She said she was still getting her life together and I got that but it certainly made me feel a way. How is it that I was managing to get myself together with some body around me, and everybody that is supposed to be dear to me can't?

This is why I have abandonment issues and keep my guard up. The shit does not make sense. I understand everybody processes stuff differently, but everybody that means the most to me has always abandoned me. That shit leaves a bitter taste in your mouth. My biological dad, Keiontay, hell my mother...I just pray my child never does. I am still trying to close my open wound, but then life doesn't stop as you're trying to heal. In the process of healing some other shit pops up, triggers me, and now the wound has grown instead of shrinking. Seems like a constant cycle that I have to figure out how to get control of.

The abandonment issues have led to mental issues. Thinking back to Keiontay, I was holding on through all the bullshit at the expense of not being abandoned again, and it still ended up happening. I'm really starting to feel like my best isn't good enough. Sometimes when you are alone with your thoughts you can go back and forth a million times of who the blame should fall on. But any who...

I wanted to reach out to the one person I felt like I still could despite her physical absence. I had been curious why we hadn't been hearing from her as much so I called. Boy oh boy did I get my ass handed to me and wish I never had.

"Hey Mom!" I said with some excitement in my voice at the chance to hear her voice.

"Hey Nova, I'm sorry I haven't been coming to see you guys, but I will change that soon. Things have settled down and I will be able to travel a little more now," she explained.

"Travel a little more? Where have you been staying Mom? What is going on with you? Like you have semi been ghosting us with how inconsistent you have been. I call and you don't return the call, I text but you don't text back, or you text back days later, not very long facetime calls." Nova rattled off.

"Nova, my life does not revolve around you. It's bad enough your father was no good, so a lot fell on me and now I am trying to regain my own independence. Plus with you being selfish, there was no room for me to grow. The whole time before you got your place you were just focused on getting you and Nolan somewhere to live. Not once did you ever consider my feelings. You didn't even try to get enough bedrooms to include me. Not factoring in If I wanted to come and live with you guys, knowing damn well I don't have anybody," her mom expressed.

Feeling confused, "Mom....you think I was being selfish to focus on getting my baby and I a place to stay? That is crazy and all my credit and finances approved me for was a two bedroom. Plus you were out before we even moved in so what are you talking about?"

"Nothing Nova, I just see how I raised you must have gone out of the window. It's okay. Thanks to my friend, I have managed to get on my feet, get some money coming in, and be able to get my own place. So no, I have not been in a rush to come and see you guys because I really was mad at you, but I'm over it now. You have to live your life, I understand. It's my fault for thinking I could depend on you," her mother said.

"I am shocked as hell right now."

"For what? Now you know," her mom said.

"You're making it seem like my choice to be responsible is wrong. You're acting like you don't know what I was going through. Then in the struggle, you put in no effort to help me find a place, wouldn't work or nothing!"

"It's not my fault you chose the wrong man and he left you! I am your mother. I gave birth to you and you put me second, I am supposed to always be a priority, and it seems like you have forgotten that. And why would I help when it's your job to help look after me. You know I just lost your step dad and he was my only source of income. Did you once ask me how I was? If I was okay? No, everything was just you you you, but it's okay honestly. Let's put this all past us and move forward. Some people are too inconsiderate and selfish to see their own mistakes. I had to realize that and let my passion fall," her mom replied.

"Keiontay has nothing to do with this conversation. It's funny how you believe I was or am the problem, but at least that explains the semi ghosting. Well now I know it was actually a cold shoulder."

"I'm not going to go back and forth with you. I said what I felt, gave an update on my life, and addressed the past how you wanted. Now where is my handsome grandson? I should be coming to see him some time this month," she said.

Laughing slightly, “so you expect me to get over what you just said now because you’re over it?”

“I mean you don’t have to, I just no longer want to talk about it, and I am not. It’s your life. So is he sleeping? I want to see him,” she said.

“Oh, yeah no he isn’t and you cannot. You might not want to talk about it, you can hang up if you want, but I am going to speak my damn peace. I am baffled but feel disrespected. How do you even let the words selfish leave your mouth when it comes to my child and getting my life together for him? It’s a whole ass contradiction to say you want to see him, but felt it was selfish of me to get him and I a home. Like that does not even make sense”

“I see you must not be feeling good because you’re trying to start with me, and I am not the one you should be mad at. I bet you haven’t snapped at Keiontay. Probably haven’t even heard from him, and here you are raising your voice at me. The woman that gave you life and stuck beside you during your pregnancy, and I wasn’t even the one that knocked you up. Girl redirect your anger at who you are really mad with,” she responded.

Unsure of what further to say as her mother redirected everything on her. Nova lied and said Nolan needed to be changed to get off the phone and end the call.

What was going on in my life? My child's father basically left me because I wouldn't let him no longer have his way. My mom basically tried to make me feel like I am a bad person for putting my child first. Like I have struggled at times to hold my tongue cause my mouth can get vicious, but fuck it at this point. I will just ignore people. Because anybody that tries to make it seem like being responsible and standing up for myself was the wrong thing to do are the type of people that do not need to be in my life. That is some narcissistic and manipulative bullshit. When you start setting boundaries for people that are used to walking over you, they get mad. Make it seem like you are the problem. I am no longer falling for that shit. I don't care who you are, my peace will no longer be compromised to appease other people's happiness and depreciate my own.

My son is one of the only reasons I do not feel alone in this world at this point. Some days it's hard to stay strong, but for him I will fight on because I for sure am all he has at this point. The other reason is shockingly Omar. Hell it shocked me too, but sometimes in life the oddest things can bring people together I guess. The once ass hole that I called him has become a great friend of mine. He called me one day to check on Nolan and I. It was during a time where money was lagging but I still needed to come through. Mentally it was draining me trying to pull a two person role alone. Nolan wasn't feeling good, my light bill had almost tripled on me, a disconnection was nearing, diapers were low, and plus Nolan's first birthday was coming up.

Who was I to turn to with all this? I thought about taking out a loan, but loan interests and the time frames they were offering had me in over my head. I would much rather pay the system then ask people for help because people will ask more questions to be in your business than to actually help you. So I am one that tries to avoid that at all points. With being at a breaking point of trying to keep it all together plus maintain his daycare fees, I was about to blow. I couldn't call my mother, well I could have and I did but it didn't matter. I thought about my cousin, but reaching out to her or any other part of my family would lead to a plethora of questions. Where was his father, when am I putting him on child support, them wanting to talk to him ......blah blah no shit I wanted to hear and it certainly was not going to help a damn thing.

So the day when I felt I was about to fall apart and Omar called, I answered the phone with an attitude. I knew he was about to come with some bullshit as usual but I was wrong. I don't remember the conversation word for word, but I know my first words were, "What are you calling for some pussy? You still are not getting it, and I really wish you stop pretending like you care just so you can try and get between my legs."

Nova shook her head at herself as she started laughing. I was so rude. Besides that one date at the very beginning of us meeting, that I hardly acknowledge because it was so long ago. I was just so unfortunately used to that being all it was with him besides the occasional phone calls. I was on edge. Plus what I was already going through, but I was wrong. Even if I wasn't when I started crying nothing else mattered. He became immediately concerned with what was wrong with me. To cry in front of anyone or even on the phone was something I rarely did, but in that moment it was so much that I could not hold back. After insisting to tell him what was going on, I was stunned at how he listened. Not only did he listen but he asked if he could take care of it all. He just needed until tomorrow to get it all done so that could help take the burden off of me a little. It felt good to hear and it calmed my nerves, but believing that he actually would was something I doubted.

The next day came around 2:30pm in the afternoon. I was getting off work and about to go pick up my son. He texted and asked if he could meet me or if meeting me at my place would be better. I was unsure what to say. I stalled by taking a minute to check my notifications that had piled up. Because seeing him was something I was not sure if I was ready for.

However, the multiple emails from my power and phone company paused the decision. When bills are behind, a nerve wrecking thing is getting those emails that contain disconnections or extra late fees. I just knew that was what I was about to open, but I was wrong. It was a notification letting me know that my bills had been paid, and when the next bill would be due. I was confused. Like who could have, I started to think but then the crazy hopeless romantic side of me was like maybe it was Omar. I had told him, but I didn't believe he would. Then again he wants to see me, so it would make sense.

In no mood for guessing games because I was thankful for the blessing. God knows I was because that was a weight lifted off of me that I needed. I started to cry because I felt like I could breathe a little. That blessing gave me a head start to get things back on track.

As I started my car, I called Omar and connected him to my bluetooth so I could be hands free as I drove to get my son.

"Hey there!" he said as he answered on the first ring.

"Hey, umm, did you by chance pay my light and phone bill? Because I got emails saying paid, wait, maybe it's an error in their system," she said. Immediately starting to feel embarrassed.

"Nova, it's no error, yes I did," he said.

"Wait, wow, umm....I don't know what to say," she said feeling baffled.

"Say nothing, you don't owe me any thanks or anything. All I wanted you to know was that I heard you, and let you know that I am not the guy you think I am," he explained.

"But, why now?" she questioned.

"Nova, when have you ever told me you needed help? I can't read your mind. I can imagine being a single mother isn't easy, but stepping in where I am not needed is something I don't do. Plus, I have always known you to hold shit down in all honesty."

"I hear you, and I do but sometimes, shit in life happens," she said.

"It does, and that's okay. I am here for you whether you believe it or not. I might not show it but I am. Sometimes it's hard for me to express myself, but I thought checking on you here and there clearly showed my interest in you still."

"I mean, I felt you were interested but in my vagina more so than me to be real with you. Every time we linked, it was always sex, sex, sex ,and nothing else. Plus you dip directly after giving, hit it and quit it vibes," she explained.

"We did go on a date once, so it wasn't all just sex, and I do apologize. I was protecting myself to keep it a buck with you. I figured that as long as I kept our interactions short I would not catch feelings, but in minutes of seeing your face I was already in love. Then you surprised me within just a little time of knowing me, blew my mind because no female had ever. Hell, no family member has ever."

"Oh yeah, that one long ass time ago, but that is crazy. This sounds like a dream. I feel like you are pulling my leg. Why not show me this side of you in the beginning instead of just smashing and dipping? Because that presents the complete opposite of now."

"That's what I was used to unfortunately. Smashing and dipping. Most women never had a problem with it, just as long as I came through and put it down."

"So you thought I was the same?"

"Honestly, I felt something about you was different, but I kept my guard up despite that, cause I was waiting for the other shoe to drop. So I just did my fuck boy shit. But every time I left your spot, I felt like it was wrong. I started not wanting to disappoint you. Then I started to realize that you weren't interested in just sex from me and my looks. So, in order to give you a better version of me and the man you deserve, I distanced myself. My intention was to continue to reach out to let you know I was still interested however."

"Wow!" was all Nova could manage to say.

"So, when I called to do my normal check in and you started crying it was either now or never to let you know that I can be the man that you need. I'm not perfect. I have some healing to continue to do, but I hear you and I am here for you Nova Emerson."

Wiping the tears that were building in her eyes before she spoke, “You know my last name?” she said as her voice trembled as she tried to stop from crying.

“Of course, but I want to get to know more about you, if that’s okay with you?”

As silence filled the phone, Nova heart raced as she pulled into the parking lot of the daycare, parked and just sat there for a minute.

“Hello, are you still there?”

“Yeah, just processing everything.”

“I understand, do you want me to meet you at your place, or do you want to meet me before y’all head in?” he asked.

“I would much rather you come when Nolan is asleep, so can you come by once I get him down for bed?” she asked.

“That’s fine, do you want me to order y’all some food or are you straight?”

Shaking her head, she scratched her head and said no.

“Okay,well just call me when you want me to head that way.”

“Okay,” she said and ended the call.

CHAPTER 8

On the way home, Nova stopped to grab her and Nolan dinner. Yes, Omar had offered, but she was struggling to wrap her head around his actions. For so long, she has been the giver, that someone giving her felt strange. Especially with her and his history. The unexpected turn of niceness had her feeling conflicted with happiness and hesitation.

While in the line waiting for their order she replayed Omar's words in her head.

"So, when I called to do my normal check in and you started crying it was either now or never to let you know that I can be the man that you need. I'm not perfect. I have some healing to continue to do, but I hear you and I am here for you Nova Emerson."

Maybe he's just saying that but why? She asked herself.

I want to be happy and embrace every word, but my guard is up. She admitted to herself as she looked in the rear mirror at her son who was engrossed in his tablet watching his favorite show.

No, I never fully gave him a chance, but what chance was there to give him when time after time he showed his ass to me of only hitting me up to have sex. Yes, there was that one date so long ago, I barely remember. Yes, he's checked on me without it leading to sex here and there, but the communication always was minimal. Like what's different. I don't want to risk my heart again. I can't and I don't want Nolan seeing anybody come in and out of his life. He does not need that and neither do I, Nova thought to herself as she finally got the food and they were headed home.

As they made it home, ate, and she started to get Nolan ready for bed, she could hear her heart beating so loud she could hear it in ear. Either her blood pressure was up or she was super nervous. She had a mix of emotions. After reading Nolan a bedtime story and tucking him in, she took her a shower, got out, dried off, and put on some pajamas. While checking her phone to check the time, Omar had called.

Smiling as she saw his name, she laid across the bed and called him back.

"You called?" she said as he answered.

"I did, can I still come by?" he asked.

Shaking her head and then exhaling, "Sure."

"Okay, I will be there in about twenty minutes if that's okay."

"Yes, that is fine. Let me know when you are here."

Getting out of bed, Nova went to light her candles in the living room as she does almost every night as a part of her mommy wind down time when she isn't too tired.

Sitting on the sofa with her feet tucked under her, she strolled through her phone on social media. Looking at the time, it had exceeded the twenty minutes he had said. She immediately started to think the worse.

I knew it, just full of it, why did I even believe him, she started to say until she heard a knock on the door. Her heart fell to her stomach as she looked at the door, because he said he would let her know when he was on the way. With her not hearing from him, she creeped to the door to look through the peephole as the person knocked again.

With her heart racing she scanned the room to make sure her gun was close just in case. As she looked through the peephole there was a sigh of relief when she saw Omar standing there. Unlocking the door and taking the latch off, she opened the door, and he stood there with roses and a bottle of wine smiling.

Trying not to smile, “why didn’t you call like you said?” she asked as she looked at him.

Holding out his phone with his free hand and pressing the side of it, “my phone died and I left my charger in my other car. About the time I was coming out of the grocery store with this to call you, my phone had already died. I tried searching my car, but after realizing where it was I just hoped I remembered the address right and put it into my gps,” he explained.

Stepping to the side to insinuate that he could come in, Omar walked in and stood there waiting for her to close the door.

"What?" she asked as she stepped back and looked at him feeling confused.

"Nothing, I'm waiting for your direction," he said and started to smile.

"Oh, well you can have a seat in the living room and I will grab us some glasses.

"Cool, what about the flowers? Do you not like them?" he asked as he sat down and placed the flowers on the table.

Walking out of the kitchen starting to laugh, "well dang, let me make it back and sit down," she said as she sat down two wine glasses and a vase with water.

"Oh, you already had it, my bad," he said and started laughing.

"It's cool, it's funny honestly, cause that sounded like some I would have said, but no I love the flowers. Roses are actually my favorite."

Sitting back on the couch with one leg tucked under her as she watched him pour them both a glass of Pinot Grigio. "Not that seeing you doesn't feel nice I guess, but why the urgency to see me now?" she said.

"You guess, that's cute," he said as he handed her a glass, and took the other one. I mean seeing you feels nice, but I just wanted to give you this in person instead of digitally sending it to you. Plus, since you said later in the day then earlier, I figured why not surprise you as well."

"Give me what," she started to say as he reached in his pocket and handed her a band of twenty dollar bills.

Holding the money and looking at him feeling confused. "Why are you giving me a thousand dollars, you just paid my light and phone bill which helps a ton, so here," she said trying to give him his money back.

"You also mentioned that your son's birthday is coming up. I thought about planning it for you, but didn't want to over step so I figured that this should cover whatever you have in mind and maybe help with a few other things," he explained.

"Omar, that is sweet of you but money won't win me over."

"I'm not trying to use it too, I want you to know I'm here for you. Coming from a hard upbringing where I had to be the breadwinner mostly and a father and brother to my siblings. I understand how hard things can be. So I just wanted to help a little, and let you know that if you ever need me that I am here."

"You're sweet, just not used to this side of you."

Laughing slightly, "hell me neither but I'm growing. I don't want to be known as immature forever. I want to grow and be the best version of myself which is why I had to get myself together. Love on myself some, forgive myself for stuff I had no control over."

"I hear you, I'm working on that too," she said, keeping her responses brief.

"Don't do that, don't be short with me. I honestly want to get to know you for once. In the beginning I was too afraid to let my guard down, but I want to know about Nova. Your favorite color, what makes you sad, happy, frustrated, aspiring towards etc..hell let's just vibe. Let me show you the commitment I should have given and shown you in the beginning. I hope you'll still give me a chance. I know it may sound corny, but I hope you're still willing to try and give us a shot. Let's start out with some light where we're just vibing and enjoying each other's company. So what do you say, you in, do you have any games for us to play if you're up for it?" he asked.

Exhaling, Nova stood up and went to her entertainment center, squatted down and pulled out a connect four game.

"This is about all the board games I have. I had uno, but Nolan got a hold of them and I assure you that deck is no longer full," she said and started to laugh.

Sitting on the floor and starting to set up the game, Omar took off his shoes and got on the floor as she sat everything up.

"So us playing this game and vibing, does that mean it's a yes?"

"Let's just say that we can be on the same page, but definitely have to take things slow."

"It's okay, that works, I just want to at least make sure we have the same understanding."

"True, to communicate early the intentions of things is definitely a plus and much needed. It feels good to have some company because I was kind of having a not so good day. Just from thinking about everything, my mom and I kind of getting into it, it all just put me in an odd place. Which color do you want to be, red or yellow?"

"Well, if you want to talk about it, I'm up to listen while we play, and I'll be red."

"Maybe," she smiled as she dropped her first yellow chip in the middle.

For the first time since she first met Omar, sitting down and spending time with him felt magical. Then the time to just have fun, and talk was well needed. It had been almost a year and some change since she had just laughed and had a good time.

They got a chance to share some of their upbringing, favorite things, dreams, things they're working on, and how they both had taken some time to heal.

As the bottle came to its end, they both had a little buzz and they laughed until tears rolled out of their eyes.

"I really needed this," she said as she looked at Omar.

"Glad I could help," he said as he looked at his watch.

"Do you have somewhere to be?" she asked, feeling a sense of insecurity in the moment as she looked at him.

"No, I was just thinking that it was getting late for you. I don't know if you have to go to work or what your plans are so I was going to head out if you wanted me to."

"I do have to work tomorrow, but I wouldn't mind you staying until morning," she said.

"That's cool," he said, starting to smile.

"Don't show all thirty two of your teeth, mister man. You are not about to get any ass over here buddy," she explained.

Starting to laugh, "Ha ha, very funny. That is not why I was smiling nor was that what I was thinking. I was actually laughing because I wanted to be respectful but I really didn't want to leave."

"Wait, are you on the run or do you just need a place to stay? Like go ahead and spill the tea now! I can't take no surprises, nobody tracking you, or in my dms coming to me as a woman. I have gone through that one time and that's enough."

Taking her hand and pulling her to him, "I have not worked my ass off to ride the coattail of no woman. If anything, I would look to add to your life not take away from you. And no flex at all, but I have two cars, a townhouse, and my family house that I maintain for my brother and sister. So I'm good on having a place to lay my head and getting around. Then like I mentioned earlier, taking the time to focus on myself really was a priority. Plus, I honest to God still wanted you, so naw, I'm good on all possible negativity."

"Well excuse me then," she said, stepping out of his embrace and heading to her bedroom. "Thank you for that explanation Mr. Russell. I appreciate you having your shit together. I don't want to leave you here by yourself, but I really need to lay down for about a few hours, so I can have some energy for work."

"That's cool, I understand," he said as he followed behind her to her bedroom.

Nova pulled back her covers and got in the bed and Omar followed suit and did the same thing.

"I don't mind you laying on my chest until you fall asleep if you want," he suggested.

Taking him up on his offer, she rolled over and laid in the cuff of his arm as he held her. Before he knew it, she was out, and he was not far behind.

As the sun rose, she rolled to her side of the bed, and Omar was still sleeping in the same spot with his arm left extended for her. It was time for her to get up and start getting Nolan ready for daycare and herself ready for work. Almost every morning she had got into the routine of waking up around six in the morning to start her day. Today that timing was off as she went to check her phone for the time. The instagram notification with a message request from @WinningSmileG had her rolling her eyes because only one person came to mind when she saw the letter G.

"What the hell man?" Nova thought to herself as she stared at her phone and contemplated if she should open it or not. "Maybe it's about Keiontay," she thought. "But what should I care, wait no, just because he's not holding down his responsibilities doesn't mean I don't have the right to care. Wait, his mom would probably tell me if anything, shit'd then probably not. A hater will likely tell you some shit quicker than people you know."

In no mood to play the guessing game when it came to Ginger, Nova decided to open the message because she felt it was better to be in the known than the unknown. Too often sweeping things under the rug can actually lead to tripping and that is not what she wanted to do. Things in her life might not have been the best, but not having her disturb her life was definitely peaceful, so this stir was one she wanted to nip in the bud.

@WinningSmileG: Nova, I hope you're happy. Keiontay hasn't been to see Kaleigh and he no longer talks to me. I hate the day he ever met you because my life would have been perfect if it wasn't for you. I am over here fighting depression because I can't see this man. I can't get in contact with him how I want to... all because whatever you did has now caused him to flee to wherever. I don't appreciate that. Can you at least give me his new number? I'm sure he still keeps in contact with you. You probably told him to not talk to me and Kaleigh. I thought you cared about her. How do you live with yourself keeping her dad from her? He was the dad she knew most, she's learning to love Tarven, but fuck it, you just ruined everything. At least for Kaleigh's sake, who you so called claim to care about deserves to talk to him.

@WinningSmileG: I know you're going to see these messages, don't be a selfish ass bitch and try to just make sure your child has a father.

@WinningSmileG: Bitch, I'm not going to beg you. I tried asking his fucking family, but they of course won't talk to me. At least the bitch who ruined everything for me can try to make something right. That's the least you can do.

@WinningSmileG: And tell me where he is! His social media isn't saying much. Like I need to talk to him, it will help me. Please. I feel like I'm going crazy, I need him.

"What the fuck?" Nova said out loud as she put her phone face down in frustration not realizing Omar had got up.

"What's wrong?" he asked, startling her.

Turning around to him standing in the door frame looking at her, "Good morning, I didn't realize you had got up."

"I'm an early riser for the most part. Kind of used to it with having to be on call so much, but you didn't answer my question. It doesn't look like your morning is starting off so good," he said.

Turning to face him, "it's nothing, just some old stuff that I thought was behind me." Exhaling, "I have to finish getting us ready for today. I will be okay," she said as she started to head in the bedroom trying to brush past Omar who continued to stand in the door frame.

Grabbing her hand before she could make it fully into the bedroom, "Nova, you won't be late for work and the baby will get to daycare on time. In essence to be the best mother you can be, and employee that involves making sure you're straight mentally and physically. I don't know how you were handling the situation before, but you agreed we would try. So don't brush me off as whatever it is as nothing because your face and body language reads differently. And it pisses me off quite frankly. Not you, but whatever it is that's so powerful that it can come through your phone and affect you like this," he said as he turned her face to him.

Dropping her head, she let his hand go and went to sit on the edge of her bed. As she sat on the bed, he came and sat on the floor in front of her.

"Why are you sitting on the floor?" she asked, noticing he didn't sit on the bed beside her.

"Because I want you to see that you have my attention," he said as he looked up at her.

Exhaling before she started to speak, "Of course, last night I wanted to keep everything in a happy place. I was enjoying smiling, laughing, and just being sincerely happy at that moment. For so long, I've smiled on the outside, but still suppressed sadness. This is why the need to heal was necessary. The scar of pain and heartache is still a work in progress, as some stuff still bothers me. Ginger is Nolan's father's ex-girlfriend. That was a lot to say, but yeah, she and him were talking before he and I met. We addressed that he was single and so was I, but not according to her. After asking me to be his girlfriend and then revealing he had a baby on the way made sense why she may have felt that way. It was my fault to continue to talk to him with such a large red flag waving in my face. So it's like I honestly brought this all on myself," she said, dropping her head feeling the urge to cry.

Moving even closer, "hey, we all make mistakes and some mistakes are needed to make us better. In my opinion, they aren't even mistakes. Just obstacles that help bring out our strengths we didn't realize we had. So go on, wait, what time does the baby have to be at daycare?"

"At the latest 9a.m. but it'll be okay, he usually gets up by 8:15 a.m. if I don't wake him up."

"Okay cool, go ahead just wanted to make sure."

"Thank you, and long story short, when she found out he had moved on, she tried to reach out. I thought she was being genuine, I was wrong. Since then she's being cyber bullying me, stalking me, trying to get me fired, just harassing the fuck out of me trying to make my life miserable. I even unfortunately shot at her once. I was so fed up because she pulled a gun on me, messed up my car, the list goes on. He and I aren't together anymore. Haven't been in a year and some change and she just messaged me this morning. After everything hit the fan about her lying to him, she still blames me as the reason everything that she wanted with him didn't go as planned. I had finally gotten okay with not looking over my shoulder every minute and laying low to stay out of the way. Once Nolan was born, I wanted to kill all the drama that I never wanted anyway. So just her reaching back out after all this time just bothers me, because why? I don't know where he is, I don't talk to him, nothing! It makes no sense, like leave me alone," she said as a tear rolled down her face.

CHAPTER 9

Standing to his feet and immediately sitting next to her to hold her, "Hey, I know it might be hard for you to accept it at first, but no more do you have to go through this by yourself. My only concern is, where was your help, what did he do to fix any of this? Has he tried checking her any? And what do you want to happen? Just tell me these things and I will act accordingly. Because I promise to you Nova Emerson, even in our distance, I never once stopped thinking about you. I be damned, if anyone tries to hurt you or your son. I can and will show you that I am a man of my word," he expressed as he kissed her forehead and continued to hold her in his arms.

Sitting up out of his embrace and wiping her tears, "help, umm, at one point I reached out to my cousin AC up in Syracuse. I ended up discovering that the little girl who Ginger claimed to be his, wasn't. I had intentions to do something bad, but finding that out detoured me because I didn't want to hurt him. Immediate family wise, I didn't want to get them involved and honestly, we're not that close. My mom knew about the situation, but didn't really help much. She just did a lot of talking and that kind of made things more so worse than better. As for him...in a sense he blamed me and said I started it all. That it was my fault for opening her message in the first place when he told me not to. I just want her to leave me the hell alone. Like I am not with the man, why continue to bother me?"

"You went in with good intentions. Just because you weren't aware her intentions weren't does not mean you're at fault. You can not control another grown person as he obviously couldn't either. Sorry you don't have the family support that you need. Lastly, I have to know before I help make things better....do you still love him?"

"The first time he dipped out, it hurt like hell. I was confused and wondered how I could fix things. I cried terribly, feeling like I failed my son, and like I didn't try enough. This past year's absence and complete disconnect in a sense hardened my heart. At first, I blamed myself again and questioned if I should have just let him have his way. Then I realized I would be compromising my growth I had developed in learning to stand up for myself. So as the months rolled on, the love I once had faded. Because I would be trying to convince somebody to love me for one, and two he too walked out on me. I am sick and tired of people walking out on me with no thought to look back. Then to walk out on life you created, I have no respect for you."

"I hear that, but what do you mean about him walking out too?"

"My biological dad, he's alive but could care less if I'm even alive and doesn't know a damn thing about me. I can assure you the man probably doesn't even know when my birthday is, just like Keiontay doesn't know a damn thing about Nolan. So that there was enough! I refuse to tolerate being walked out on over and over, when I'm trying to give nothing but love and understanding."

"I feel that, well I'm proud of your growth and realizing that you do deserve to be treated with respect, love, and appreciated. However, it's time for people that have caused you trouble to start seeing the consequences of their actions," he expressed.

"I don't want to make things worse Omar, I just want to be left alone. I'm taking care of my son, and I'm not bothering anyone. I just want us to be happy and left alone."

"I understand that and you're doing a great job as a mother. However, people like his so-called ex is a person that has become fixated with you. She feels you were the one that got in the way instead of holding him accountable. Either way it's no excuse. Any information that you have about her or even what she looks like I would like to know, and we can go from there. As for your ex, I don't want to linger on that but I do suggest at least putting him on child support. If you're comfortable with that, if not cool, it's just a thought. You know what actually, let life continue to deal him his hand. I will do for your son myself. If you're open to it because I had a half ass dad, which to me was still not good enough and no child deserves such bullshit."

"I don't want to be a burden to anybody. I thank you, but I decided to keep him so it's on me."

Turning Nova to him and demanding that she look at him, "Nova......I hate the pain people have caused you has made you feel like you're a burden. I promise, this is me offering and asking to be a part of y'all life. So there's no such thing as you being a burden. Let me step in! Just because you decided to be a mother and the man couldn't handle his responsibilities does not mean that's your end and you have to do it alone. I have never been a Dad, but raising my brother and sister, I damn near had to play the roles of both parents a lot of times."

"Okay," she said as she looked at him and saw the sincerity in his eyes. "I just don't want to hurt anybody or make things worse."

Laughing slightly, "Nova, you have to stop putting everybody's happiness before your own. Plus, you can't hurt someone who isn't a part of your life. Before, I can get the hesitation while you two were together, but you are no longer together. He is no longer with her, you say the love is gone...so there's no further need to be considerate and sparing. Do what you have to do to protect your peace and happiness. You deserve that just like anybody else. As far as making things worse, the best way to stop things from getting worse is to put an end to it, and that's exactly what is going to happen."

"Okay....."

"I know it feels unusual, but I got you. The both of you."

"So now what," she asked.

"You get your beautiful self ready for work, your son ready for daycare, go on about your day, and let me handle the rest. I'm off for the weekend unless I get called in."

"That sounds so simple," she said as she stood to her feet.

"When you finally have somebody in your corner, it can be. It's time to make sure you're happy all around," he said as he looked at her as she began to go through her dresser for clothes.

"Okay, so what are you about to do while I'm at work?"

"Handle business, and I'm going to go ahead and leave before the baby wakes up until you're ready for us to meet."

"I mean at this point, I kind of feel like you deserve to meet him as much as you used to call and check on him. Plus he needs to get up anyway if I want to make it even close to being on time for the both of us."

"I mean if you feel like it, I wouldn't mind it. I will just go ahead and put my shoes back on, and grab my phone and keys so I can leave out with you guys. Kind of makes me feel good to see you off anyway."

"I would like that," she said as she turned to smile at him, and then went into Nolan's room to see if he was already up. Leaning in his crib and picking him up, he began to cry until he realized his mother was holding him. He smiled leaving Nova feeling like her heart was being squeezed to see such love staring back at her. As she held him on her shoulder and patted his back, she began to pace the floor and explain that she was about to introduce him to Omar. She knew her son might not have understood her, but she still wanted to take the time to explain that he would be seeing him around a little more.

As she finished their quick talk, she went into his closet and pulled out a pair of Levi jeans, a Ralph Lauren button down shirt, white undershirt, and some little baby loafers. Then she picked him out another outfit to pack, proceeded to change him and then she headed back to her bedroom with Nolan in her arms.

Omar looked up from his phone as he sat on the edge of the bed and smiled as Nova put Nolan down. Almost like Nolan had known Omar since forever, he walked right over to him. With a smile from ear to ear, Omar felt proud and happy to be seeing Nolan. Looking at him with joy in his eyes, "ah man, you have gotten so big that is crazy. It seems like just days ago your mom was telling me she was pregnant. I was sad at first no lie because no matter how much I wished it was for me, I knew not but it's okay. In a sense, I'm still getting a chance to be a part of your life."

As Omar continued to talk to Nolan, Nova started to get ready. She put on some black dress pants, gold diamond pointed toe flats, and a polka dot dress shirt with a bow, and accessorized with gold. She stepped back in the room to check on the two of them and Omar was continuing to sit there and admire Nolan's features. "Are you okay in there?" she asked, breaking his focus.

"I'm okay, just amazed a little. Like I never over-thought this moment so much it's crazy."

"What moment?" she asked.

"You, me....if your son would accept me...it just seems like I'm dreaming. I know you've been healing and me too, but I just feel like in a sense you waited for me. I know that's not the case, but the timing just could not have turned out better. Like I can't fully say I'm mad things went wrong for you. I'm sorry to say that but his fuck up got me wanting to go harder in this life because I now have a greater purpose. Somebody else needs me in this world, and that feels amazing. Saving people daily is a job and passion of mine, but when you get to make a difference in the life of someone close to you, it hits so much different"

"Thank you for sharing this side of you," she said as she grabbed her purse, keys, and Nolan's bags to prepare to head for the front door.

As he stood to his feet, and put Nolan down, "Thank you for giving me a chance to prove to you the man I know I can be for y'all," he said as he took Nolan's hand and they headed towards the front door.

Nova strapped Nolan in his car seat and closed the door. As she turned around, Omar pulled her to him and they hugged. Before releasing her, he kissed her on the forehead and then for the first time in a long time they kissed.

"Damn," they both said and started laughing.

"Yeahhh,let me go ahead and let you go."

"Right! You started it, but yes, let us go."

"One more kiss," he suggested as Nova started to walk to the driver's side of the car.

"I can't lie, at this moment, I can't handle it. I would probably end up jumping up and wrapping my legs around you just so I can feel like it," she expressed as she opened her car door.

"I got you feeling like that?" he said with a smirk.

"Ha ha ha, so it's just me, it's cool."

"I never said that, but it's good to know because for a minute I thought you weren't attracted to me any more," he said.

"Oh please, don't pull my leg, you didn't even believe that as it left your mouth," she said and laughed.

"Not entirely, I was riding the bench for a minute," he joked.

"Umm, you got jokes this morning I see. Well at least I didn't trade you," she joked. "What are you going to be doing while I'm at work?"

"What you miss me already?" He laughed, "But probably go check on my siblings to make sure they're straight, might stop by the fire house, look into getting that situation handled for you, but nothing for real," he said.

"Okay, be careful digging when it comes to her. Hopefully I will see you when I get off."

"Love, I put out fires for a living, a deranged person is literally the least of my worries. And you guys can come to my place or I can come back over here, either or when you get off."

"I know but I'm just saying. I don't trust her worth a damn. Just please be careful. We have to get going, and maybe I do," she said and got in the car.

"Holding my own, is one thing I for sure know how to do," he yelled out as he stepped to the side as she crunk up her car. Before she could leave, he signaled for her to roll down the window.

"Man, you're going to have us super late," she said smiling.

"Just wanted to say that your answer might be maybe, but I for sure miss you already," he expressed and began walking to his silver 2019 Jeep Wrangler Sahara. Leaving Nova to drive off blushing as she headed to drop Nolan off at daycare, and then head to work.

****

"Keiontay, you are not your Father man. It's nothing I want to continue to bring up, but you were taking care of a child that wasn't even yours because you wanted to protect her and the best for her. So I don't see how you and your Father are any way similar."

Sitting up filled with frustration, "Because my Father chose drugs over me just like I did with my own child. If I would have listened to Nova, and just trusted myself to start over and do shit the right way I wouldn't be in this position. I was filled with too much self doubt. I basically sabotaged myself!" he said with anger dripping in his voice.

"I know we're not close, but what happened?" Tarven pried.

"It really doesn't matter if you know cause I'm leaving soon anyway. Once I get my leg straight, pay buddy back his money, I'm out. I need a fresh start."

"But why run, nothing is that bad."

"For you, it isn't! You haven't lost shit, I've been through too much in this fucking city. Dude almost took my life over so damn pills and money. I got robbed of being a Father, I found love and I fucked it up, messed up my career, lost my place, yeah I need a new start. So of course you wouldn't get it."

"Wait, you went back to selling man?"

"Oh, are you judging me bro?"

"No, I was just asking because...."

"Because what? You thought I was all high and mighty, and would never do such a thing again. Yeah I know me neither. You and Ginger just assumed I had everything together. Here you was trying to tear down my life because you was envious, not knowing I was fucking it up myself."

Silence filled the room as Tarven was unsure of how to respond because he honestly had never considered the triumphs Keiontay was going through.

"Yeah I know, it ain't shit to say behind that," Keiontay said as he looked at his phone debating on whether he should call Nova or not when Tarven left.

"Man, I hate seeing you like this....don't leave GA for real. There's nothing you're going through that can't be worked through. And when it comes to Nova, I'm sure she still loves you and would much rather have you around than away from the both of them."

"I hear you, but I don't feel it! I can't see my way out of this situation and I'm not about to stress myself with trying to figure out how to fix it all. I will much rather just wipe my slate clean my way and start over. Do what I know I can do."

"But if you know you can do it, why not do it here?"

"Too many memories, people I've hurt, and people that have hurt me."

"I guess I get that," Tarven said as he paused slightly to look around the room and noticed that the Keiontay he once knew was like he was no longer. "Man, I can't lie, I don't feel like you're being yourself. Don't leave your son behind like that! Maybe try getting you some help because we've been through some shit in this life. I have never seen you so down like this before," he expressed.

"Woww, isn't that the pot calling the kettle black! As one of the reasons my life feels like it fell apart suggesting I should go and get some help! That's wild G! I think it's about time you leave."

"I didn't mean no harm man, I just want you in a better head space. I've seen you bounce back and know you can do it, but I will respect your request and let you rest," he said as he stood to his feet about to leave. "Do you need anything before I head out?" he asked.

"Naw, I'm good, whatever I need I will figure it out," Keiontay said with a coldness in his voice.

Tarven shook his head as he headed towards the door. Feeling as if a part of him had failed, he dropped his head and went out the door. A part of him wanted his friend back, but to know that his selfishness and envy destroyed not only their friendship but his supposed brother too, made him feel worse than he initially did. Now there was no one he could tell about it because saying something would only create problems neither of them needed. To tell Ginger would only lead her to looking for Keiontay, Keiontay more miserable, and him back on the chase for the woman he loves.

As Tarven made it back to his car, he sat there for a minute debating if he should go back up and try again. He knew in his heart that would only be a waste, and decided to leave and head home.

CHAPTER 10

As Tarven left out of the door, Keiontay felt the urge to pee and stood up to rush to the bathroom as he normally does, but failed to remember his injury. In trying to hold his balance he ended up falling back onto the bed, as pain shot all over his body.

“Ahhh!” he cried out as a single tear rolled out of his eye. He tried to breath through the pain, but realized he was up for a challenge that he did not see coming. As he sat up feeling down on himself, he still needed to pee. At another attempt to make it but at a snail's pace, he realized he would likely not. As he used his crutches to make it around the bed to the frame of the bathroom, he no longer could hold it, and ended up peeing on himself.

As one of his crutches glided in his own urine, he almost lost his balance. Frustrated, he threw down one of the crutches and made it to the toilet forcing most of his weight on the one remaining crutch. Feeling embarrassed from peeing on himself he looked at the shower and contemplated if he should attempt to shower to wash the pee off of him. As he shook his head no, the best bet was to just make it back to the bed.

"If I could just get my clothes off and make it to the bed, I will just lay there naked for a while because this here is some bullshit," he thought to himself as he heard the notification on his phone go off.

As he sat on the toilet trying to gather his thoughts, the curiosity of who could be reaching out had him curious.

"Who could be texting me? Nobody really has my number," he thought to himself as another notification chimed. Focusing on the desire to check his phone, he sat up on the toilet, dropped his crutch on the ground next to the toilet, and started taking his clothes off. He took his shirt off with ease, but bending down to take his pants off without falling is where he ran into a problem.

As his phone went off again with another notification he grew agitated and started to drift down the road of self pity and regret. "If I had just taken Nova up on what she offered, I wouldn't be in this situation. Like what was I thinking getting back in this lifestyle? I told myself once I got out the first time I wasn't going back. I'm a fuck up for sure! I can't get shit right, then I push everyone away so much that I don't have anybody. I can't even call anybody, or trust someone would come see about me. I'm not a good father, son, boyfriend, nothing, I feel like I'll probably die by myself at this point," he thought to himself as he got mad and decided to just bend down and snatch his pants off.

Left sitting on the toilet in his brief boxers, though they were damp from his urine, he figured they would air dry. Ready to lay down, he reached down for his crutch, and proceeded to make his way back to the bed.

Sitting on the bed in his briefs, crutches leaning against the wall, he was able to finally see the messages he had received. However, he didn't recognize the number. Before he could open the message to see what it said so he could possibly figure out who it was, an unknown call was coming in causing him to shake his head.

"Ginger, you don't waste any time!" He said out loud as he just assumed it was her with him just seeing Tarven and receiving texts from an unknown number. Figuring he could use her help despite all she's done to him, he answered with more enthusiasm than he thought he would ever give her.

"I figured it wouldn't be long before you were reaching out. You must have a tracker on my ass," Keiontay said as he laughed slightly. His laughter stopped abruptly. The response that came back made his heart rate increase and made him start to look around in panic.

"I don't need to track anybody! I have enough eyes across the state that's going to always tell me what I need to know," the male voice said.

As Keiontay tried to figure out whose voice it was, it made sense why his heart rate had increased initially.

"You've been avoiding me so much that you forgot who I am huh?" the male voice responded.

"Malachi?" Keiontay asked with hesitation in his voice.

"Aw, I knew you had sense enough to remember who I was, but not sense enough to give me the respect I deserve," he said.

"No, Malachi, I respect you, I just ran into a problem and got caught up," Keiontay explained.

"Aw, how sad! You're the first person in this world to run into a problem, how crazy is that," Malachi began to say before Keiontay cut him off trying to explain.

"Malachi, I promise man, I'm going to give you back what I owe you. I just need a little more time," Keiontay started to say.

"Now Keiontay, before sending my message that I'm sure you got loud and clear, I would have doubted you. Now I strongly believe that you will, or dragging yourself to your car while leaving a trail of your own blood behind won't be possible," he stated.

"Wait, that was you?" Keiontay asked with shock in his voice.

"I figured you weren't going to die, you're strong like me just minus the common sense."

"Man, I'm sitting here barely able to walk on my own behind that shit! I was going to get you your shit back!"

"Go cry wolf to somebody who fucking believe it! When you and your pretty baby mother got into it, you hauled ass and started selling for yourself solely. Cutting me out of the equation. You started re-upping on product from one of my fucking enemies! I should have killed you the minute I found out, but I started to think about your son, and how it would lead to another young boy growing up without his Dad. Then I noticed as I watched your baby mother's apartment that he still was growing up without a Dad and you're alive. So that's when I decided to send my message and beat your ass! A part of it was for me and the other part was for your son who you're not man enough to be a fucking Father too!"

Keiontay said nothing in response to Malachi's words as he was speechless on learning the eyes that he had on him.

"Oh, cat's got your tongue! Are you mad? You hurt? You feel betrayed? Which one or all of them?" Malachi mocked Keiontay's silence.

"I fucked up," Keiontay finally admitted.

"You damn right you did, but Ima keep it real with you and admit that you fucking me over bothers me far less opposed to how you walked on that little boy! You young cats be so excited to stick your dick in almost every pretty female you see, but don't want to be accountable and responsible for the consequences that follow when you don't wrap it up! I see it so much it pisses me off! I'm that guy that's a product of my Dad walking out on me. So to prevent it, I wrap up! I don't care how good the pussy is, I'm wrapping it up. I knew every woman I slept with, I wasn't ready so I enjoyed myself but played it smart."

"So you're mad I'm not taking care of my son, but you don't want your money back?" Keiontay asked, trying to get clarification.

"At what fucking point did you hear me say I didn't want my money back? See it's that selective hearing shit that fuck a lot of people up. You so used to hearing what the fuck you want to hear that you miss the important message in general."

"No, Malachi, I'm just trying to get an understanding of the situation," he started to say before Malachi cut him off!

"I would feel sorry for you and how dense you are because you truly don't see your wrong in general, but that's okay. I'm not going to raise you! Life will do that at this point. I'm over talking to you before you further piss me off. You have 72 hours to get me back the money I loaned you. The money from the pills you owe me, I'll chalk that up as a loss cause I have sense enough to know that the cripple can only do so much! But I highly suggest you make it work before you don't get the chance to leave the state how you plan once you're fully able to walk," Malachi said and hung up the phone, not giving Keiontay a chance to respond.

"So this the shit I was could have prevented," Keiontay started to think to himself as he looked around thinking about how the room was probably bugged for Malachi to know about his plans to leave.

"I need to," he started to say out loud but remembered to choose carefully what to say out loud.

In the hopes that texting would be better, he decided to go ahead and open the texts that he was initially curious to open. Both messages had the same number and as he scratched his head while opening the first message, he managed to gain a smile within this hectic day.

+14043551111: Hey, I just wanted to check on you. I know I don't know you from a can of paint, but there is something about you that made me want to make sure you're okay.

+14043551111: I didn't even say who I was, smh...this is Morgan. I guess I'm a little nervous. I have never done anything like this before.

After reading the messages and seeing they were from the nurse that was waiting with him, he instantly knew he was going to respond. Just in that short minute her messages helped his life not seem so crazy in that moment.

"Yes, I am alive!" Keiontay texted back with a smile on his face.

Instead of texting back, the same number was calling him and he instantly answered while laughing slightly.

"Hello," he said.

"I'm not much of a big texter, but I wanted to break the ice and make sure it was actually you instead of just texting," she explained and giggled a little.

"It's cool, hearing your voice really made me feel a lot better," he said.

"Well, that's good to hear and hearing your voice isn't too bad either, but before I go, how are you feeling? I know the dose they gave you before leaving has probably worn off by now," she stated.

"I'm not sure got damn, all I know is that I don't like this shit. I feel helpless almost," he expressed.

"You only feel helpless because you're trying to do it by yourself," she said.

"Yeah I am because from what I just learned it's going to be better that way. I might struggle along the way but the less people are involved, I won't have to feel like I am letting anybody down. Or bringing hell in anyone's life any more."

"What led you to believe that you have to heal alone and think for other people?" she asked. "As humans we are given choices to choose from right or wrong. Sometimes we choose wrong but in error is when you learn most. I know you can't believe that the very things we use every day from something as simple as a sheet to the medicine they put in your veins was a success from the first go round? No. Let people choose for themselves if they want to be a part of what you have going on. You're trying to box people out without even giving them a chance and that's unfair," she explained.

"I hear you, but so much in my life seems out of place that I'm not sure where to start and who to let in," he stated.

"Nobody has everything together, so you be open and pay attention. Treat people according to how they treat you and things will be simpler. Just because somebody shows you they are an asshole, you can decide to continue to deal with them and accept what they are capable of while keeping your distance, or you can cut them off. The choice is yours and you have to stop blaming yourself for everything."

Keiontay said nothing as he took in her words and nodded his head in agreement with what she was saying.

"See, I talk too much and I have now probably scared you off," she said in response to his silence.

"Look at you being a hypocrite! You just told me not to blame myself for stuff. The minute I am sitting here processing what you're saying, you took my silence as you were talking too much," he expressed.

She started to laugh as he was right. "You're right, but I am human, which is another thing I wanted you to realize. I am human and so are you. We can have and give all the advice in the world to someone, but that doesn't make us perfect nor means we can even fully take the advice we give out. Life is a forever learning lesson, it's what we do with those lessons that shows our growth," she continued.

"Beautiful and wise! I like it!" he said.

"Hm maybe, I know a little bit here and there, but before I let you go, we both know you lied about having help. So do you need me to come by and help out a little before I head home?" she offered.

"Would you do that for me for real?" he asked feeling perplexed.

"Yes, because I know you need help and are too stubborn to ask for it...plus whoever that guy was I didn't believe you were going to let him help you how you need. It was just a free ride," she stated.

"Girl, don't act like you know me! I could be a serial killer," he said and laughed.

Laughing at his attempt at a joke, "No, I don't know you but you don't seem that hard to figure out. If you were a serial killer, you're a bad one because most of them usually do the stabbing and don't get stabbed," she said as she burst out laughing.

"Ah damn! You got jokes I see," he said and laughed slightly.

"Just a few, but I can't be on the phone much longer. My shift will be over soon, so I will reach back out," she stated.

"Cool, just let me know and I will shoot you the address," he said.

"I feel like you probably haven't eaten since you left. Would you like me to bring you something when I come?" she offered.

"Ah damn, yes! I will pay you back when you get here or I can send you the money. Either way you will get your money back."

"I didn't ask for it back, consider it me just looking out for you," she counteracted.

"No offense, but I would prefer to pay you back so please do not deny me giving you your money back. Not trying to be rude but I don't need anybody doing any favors for me at this point in my life."

"I would not ever attempt to enter your life with the intention to hold anything I do over you or against you. I hear you and will respect that. I will call once I'm off and leaving the hospital."

"I appreciate that and okay," he said and the call ended.

Morgan had distracted his mind from Malachi for a couple of minutes, but the truth was that he needed to clear up that situation. Having to constantly look over his shoulder was something that he didn't want to do.

"I'm in a bad place right now and I really just need time to get my shit together. I could hustle the money up but that would take about two weeks and my ass barely can walk to the bathroom so that's out the window. Maybe I could get Tarven to help me but I really don't trust his ass. There's no telling when Ginger will pop up and I really don't have time for that shit. To keep it all the way real with myself, I got about $7k on a debit card and about a thousand in cash. I was going to get to $10k and bounce. I guess Malachi knew what I was going to do which is why he sent his message. I can pay him his $5k and still have like $3k left, but it wouldn't leave me much time to be here. I would either have to find a cheaper hotel, a motel, or be flat out homeless until I could get some shit to shake," Keiontay thought to himself as he laid back on the bed and stared up at the ceiling.

"What to do?" Keiontay said out loud to an empty room. "I can't be broke again and I can't afford to be on the streets, especially not like this." His leg felt like he was carrying around a ton of bricks on him. It was also a quick reminder that he had to figure out his plans quickly with so much at stake. "I feel bad for even considering going this route, but to me it's a pretty smart ass option. Maybe the universe was telling me the way to go, he thought to himself. She is a nurse, she can help make sure my wound is straight and I'm healing properly. She has a good head on her shoulders, and she is already willing to step into what I got going on in a sense. Maybe if I can get my foot in the door good enough I can fix a great bit of my problems until I can get myself straight. Then again, I don't want to come off like I'm trying to use anybody. Damn man! I supposed to be doing better, trying to better myself, but I feel like there's a target on my back pulling me back into my old ways. Hell I haven't even stopped my old ways, talking about pulling me back. I feel like I'm spiraling out of control honestly. I'm stuck in between wanting to do right and being comfortable in my wrong.

CHAPTER 11

Tarven made it home, he walked in and went straight to the bathroom as his stomach had held in there as long as it could. As he sat on the toilet, Ginger came in while he was on the toilet scrolling through his phone. She stood in the door frame with her arms crossed across her chest.

"Damn, can I have some privacy?" Tarven asked as he looked up at her from his phone.

"No, the fuck you can not! Where have you been?" she asked.

"I was finishing dropping off a customer," he stated as he continued to look through his phone while trying to use the bathroom.

"Tarven, don't give me that bull shit. Since you have started doing that rideshare shit, you've usually only worked four to five hours a day. Today, you got home after me which never usually happens."

"I took on some more calls Ginger! Now close the door," he said, getting irritated.

"As soon as you come home, you come in and walk right pass me like you don't fucking see me sitting on the sofa. Then head straight to the bathroom!"

"Where is my daughter Ginger?"

"Don't try and change the fucking subject! She's in her fucking skin, that's where the fuck she is!"

"Stop playing with me man! Where is she?" he asked as he locked his phone and made eye contact with Ginger.

"I'll tell you when you tell me where you're coming from!" she demanded.

"You so fucking insecure that it's crazy! No matter how much love I give you, it doesn't fill the void of you not loving your damn self and it shows."

"Blah blah blah!" she said as she rolled her eyes.

"You act like I came in the door and went straight for the shower to wash a bitch pussy juices off me! I know that's what you used to, but as you can clearly see, I had to fucking shit! Meaning my stomach was probably hurting which is why I came in so abruptly," he explained as he started reaching for the tissue.

Walking over to him, she knocked his phone on the floor and snatched the tissue from him.

"What the fuck is wrong with you?" he yelled.

"I hate you! That's what's wrong with me!" She yelled back.

"Boo fucking who! What's the real problem cause we both know that's not true," he said as he stood up and snatched the tissue away from her.

"Tarven, I'm not happy, that is what is wrong! I'm tired of lying and pretending. Tired of being depressed, tired of going with the motions. I don't hate you, but every day I'm sad and you do nothing to try and make me feel better. I work and come home, and it's the same shit every damn day! At least Keiontay did stuff for me and we went out!" she explained.

Flushing the toilet, pulling his pants up, and headed to wash his hands, he exhaled. As he continued to wash his hands, Ginger continued.

"You're always working and always only focused on Kaleigh. You're almost just like him. Neither of you give a fuck about me. I don't see why I stay nor care about either of you pieces of shit! Y'all are sorry excuses for men!" she said with anger dripping in her voice.

Flicking the water from his fingertips, he dried his hands on the hand towel, walked over to Ginger, and grabbed her by the throat.

As she tried to take his hand from around her throat her eyes began to widen as she felt her breath being cut off.

"You talk entirely too fucking much. I told you not to compare me to him! I keep trying to show you I love you and you're an ungrateful bitch! He showed you he didn't want you and you are still standing here comparing me to him. He had no respect for you, was basically using you, and taking from you more than he was giving you. Here I am being faithful to you day in and day out, going to work, trying to be a good Dad, and that shit still isn't good enough for you."

"I can't breathe," she managed to get out as she continued to try and take his hand from around her neck.

"When I try to take you out on dates you're too tired. You're not in the mood, you got a headache, it's always something, and you want to say what the fuck I don't do for you! On my fucking soul, you are lucky my daughter is in this house! I would knock your head into the wall like I want to, but out of respect I hope this will teach your ungrateful, miserable ass to stop fucking playing with me," he said and released her.

Falling to the floor, trying to catch her breath, she felt like life was entering back into her body. She looked up at him and rage filled her. She took his phone and threw it across the room causing it to shatter in pieces.

“You just threw my phone!” he yelled.

“Fucking right I did!” she said as she stood to her feet and looked him in his eyes.

“Oh you want me to hit you huh?” Tarven said as he caught on to what Ginger was trying to do.

“If you're feeling froggy, jump then motherfucker!” Ginger egged him on.

Tarven smiled and stepped back from Ginger as he almost fell into her trap. “You know what Ginger, I’ll do you one better,” he said as he brushed past her to head to the hallway closet.

Hot on his every step, “where the fuck you think you going?” she screamed after him.

Opening the closet door and pulling out a wooden baseball bat, Ginger jumped back but still spoke with anger in her voice. “You think that’s supposed to scare me! I want you to hit me bitch!” she yelled and continued to follow him as he headed towards the front door.

“You want me to show my ass! I got you love!” he said as he opened the front door and ran towards her car.

“Tarven you better not touch my fucking car!” she yelled as she stood in the door frame of the front door.

"Okay, okay, okay, I'm sorry! I can't afford that right now!" she yelled in hopes he would not follow through.

"Fuck your sorry!" he said as he walked around to the passenger side of her car and busted the passenger side windows with two hits.

"Tarven stop!" she yelled.

"Selfish ass!" he yelled as he knocked her side mirrors off, and beat in the hood of the car. "Nothing is never good enough for you!" he yelled as he beat in her headlights and then the driver's side windows.

Screaming to the top of her lungs for him to stop! "Don't make me call the police!" she yelled.

"Do what you need to!" he screamed as he beat at the back window until he shattered it and he finally stopped.

With a sinister grin on his face, he dropped the bat and started to head into the house as Ginger stood in the door with shock on her face and her mouth dropped.

"Pick your mouth up before I put something in it," he said as he brushed past her and started laughing.

Ginger closed her mouth, but continued to stand there perplexed as to what she was going to do about her car. There was no way insurance was going to cover those damages, but in the midst of her concern about her car, a part of her was turned on.

"I knew he cared for me, but damn," she said to herself as she stepped backwards in the house and closed the door.

Tarven was sitting on the couch drinking a beer and watching tv. As she gathered her words of what to say to him, he spoke before she could say anything.

"Ginger come in here and sit down! Luckily Kaleigh is still sleeping through all that bullshit! I just want to relax at this point. Coming home and having to show my ass is something I had no intentions to do nor was in the mood for, but I had to show you to stop testing me," he said.

"You're right babe and I'm sorry," she said as she stood in front of him and began to straddle his lap.

"What are you doing Ginger?" he asked as she fully straddled him and took his beer out of his hand and placed it on the floor.

She started to kiss on his neck and suck on his ear as she grinded her hips on his growing erection.

"That shit turned me on," she said as she kissed his neck and then his lips.

Kissing her back, he grabbed her by the throat and she smiled as they looked each other in the eyes.

"Man you crazy!" he said as they continued to stare each other down.

"And so are you, but I love it," she said as she stood up, reached in his pants, pulled his throbbing thick erection out, and took off her leggings.

As she re-straddled him, she pulled her panties to the side, took his erection and inserted it inside her as they continued to look each other in the eyes.

He bit his lip as she began to bounce on his lap enjoying every inch of him inside of her. Smacking her ass as she bounced made her bounce harder and their moans grow louder.

In the middle of catching her nut, she stood up leaving Tarven with a face of confusion, and asking, "what are you doing?"

"Taking my panties fully off, I know you don't think I'm finished," she said as she took her panties, shirt and bra off.

Following Ginger's lead he took his shirt, boxers, and pants off fully and before he could get his shirt fully off, Ginger was re-inserting his erection. As he moaned with satisfaction she leaned in and bit him on the neck causing him to grip her ass aggressively.

Taking one of her breasts in his mouth, Ginger screamed out as she came. As she collapsed on his chest he lifted her up and bent her down with her face in the sofa and her ass in the air.

Before re-inserting himself inside of her, he dropped to his knees and planted his face between her pussy lips. Gliding his face from her clitoris to her vagina caused her to shake and beg him not to stop.

"Don't stop! Fuck yes," she said barely above a whisper as she grinded her pussy on his face.

Smacking her ass as he stood to his feet, she moaned as he inserted himself causing her to cum again.

"That's right, keep cumming on this dick! I know you love it," he said as he watched the jiggle of her ass as she threw it back on him.

Slowing his strokes before he pounded in and out of her, he smacked her ass again, but this time he came inside her. As he wiped the sweat off his forehead, she turned around, got on her knees on the sofa, and licked the nut off his dick causing him to tremble slightly.

Stepping back from her and sitting on the other side of the sofa away from her, he closed his eyes trying to catch his breath.

"Damn girl!" he managed to get out.

Sitting on the sofa, leaning her head back, she said, "we needed that."

"Hell yeah!" he responded.

It had been months since they had been intimate, and despite her busted car windows and his broken phone, in that moment they were happy. Tarven contemplated if he should bring up running into Keiontay or keeping it to himself.

He loved Ginger, but he knew a part of her heart still belonged to Keiontay. To know he was back in town was something he was unsure if he should tell her because he knew it could mean losing her again. It sounds corny, but the thought of being selfish with the woman he loved was something he didn't second guess. Plus it was not like him and Keiontay was fully on good terms again, and would be hanging out like they used to. But he wanted to tell somebody of the day he had, and Ginger was his go to person.

As she continued to lay her head back on the sofa embracing the moment she reached for Tarven's hand and he received it, and it made him smile. However, he was conflicted because since he and Ginger got together fully, he promised himself to be honest, loyal, and communicate as effectively as possible. As they continued to hold hands, he took in the silence and had to be realistic with himself. He could not control the situation any more than Ginger could. He was preaching to her, but needed to take his own advice. No matter how in love with her he was, he had to accept that her choosing him had to be natural.

"This woman got me fucked up to the point, I den turned into a bitch. Out her busting windows and shit like a hoe throwing a temper tantrum," he thought to himself. "I got to do better. If she leaves me and goes to search for him, that will just show the truth of what she really wants. With true love, it's not forced, manipulation, control, and it surely isn't abuse and anger," he continued to think.

"I saw Keiontay today," he blurted out, breaking the silence in the room.

As soon as those four words left his mouth, she let his hand go and sat straight up.

With shock on her face, "like face to face?" she asked as she looked at him with her eyes wide awaiting his response.

Scratching his head, he sat up and leaned forward, "yes," he confirmed.

"Oh my goodness! Like how was it? How did it happen? What did you two talk about? When did he get back?" she asked as a smile emerged on her face more with almost every question.

"Well, somebody seems excited as fuck," he said dryly and stood to his feet. "I'm about to go take a shower," he said and started to head to the bathroom.

"Wait," she yelled out and began to run behind him. "You don't start telling me about running into your best friend who you haven't spoken to in about a year and some change and not tell me how it went."

As he leaned in to turn on the water while he grabbed him a towel and washcloth, "I'm sure you're very concerned about his and I friendship Ginger," he said as he moved the shower curtain back preparing to get in.

Grabbing his arm before he could get in, "don't be like that babe, I just want to know."

Pulling away from her grip and getting in the shower, he stuck his head out and said, "I'll tell you but I want to finish my shower first."

"I understand, I can just sit here on the toilet until you're done and that way I can hear you still, or I can wash up in the sink."

"Whatever Ginger," he said as he realized he had opened up a can of worms. There was no chance of him putting the lid back on that can without her badgering him all night.

"So what were you doing when you ran into him," she inquired, trying to get the story out of him.

"What I'm not doing is telling her ass every detail. I can be honest and let life run its course. I don't have to give her every damn step by step to the dude. Cause I know she will leave both Kaleigh and I high dry if she comes across his ass," Tarven thought to himself as he listened to Ginger pry.

"Did you hear me babe?" she asked.

"Now I'm babe," Tarven thought to himself and started laughing.

"What's so funny?," she asked.

"Nothing, but naw it wasn't a run into situation per say. I was about to clock out cause it was around my normal time. Plus I had to shit but the system had already added the rider to my queue so I just said fuck it, and would make that my last one. Then I looked at the name and was like naw, I just have to be tripping, and if so why would he be at the hospital if it was him," he started saying until she cut him off.

"Hospital? Was it him? Why was he at the hospital?" she inquired.

"Damn, you gone let me finish or are you going to keep interrupting me?" he asked.

"My bad, just trying to get the full just of what happened."

"Bet, anyway, so long story short, it was him, he wanted to cancel the ride all together. I told him that since I was already there that I could go ahead and take him home.......yada yada ya. I helped him in the house, I apologized, he accepted it, said what we did fucked him up, and I asked him if he needed me to stay longer to help him. He said no, and I dipped out. End of story."

"Wait, back the hell up," she said as she turned the water off and wrapped up in a towel and went to stand by the shower until Kaleigh started crying.

"Is that Kaleigh?" he asked as he turned the water off to see if he was hearing right.

"Yes, but I was trying to understand," she started to say before he cut her off.

"Ginger, please don't make me say what I'm thinking. I promise, I will answer what you want to know to the best of my ability," he said and turned the water back on to finish his shower.

Ginger rolled her eyes and went to check on their daughter. About fifteen minutes passed, Kaleigh had stopped crying and Ginger had put on clothes and was sitting on the bed scrolling through her phone while their daughter was sitting in the middle of the bed eating cheerios while watching cartoons.

As Tarven finally came out of the bathroom with a towel wrapped around his waist, she looked up from her phone and blushed as she looked at him.

Laughing slightly, he asked, "what are you smiling at?"

"Nothing babe, just seeing something that I like," she said.

"Girl, don't try and butter me up for the rest of the story."

"Well since you brought it up, I wouldn't mind you holding up what you promised before I left the bathroom."

"Cool," he said as he started to search through the dresser drawers for some boxers and pajamas.

"So, um is he in bad shape? Like from a cold type of bad shape or a bad fight?" she inquired.

As he continued to get dressed, “um not really, it’s actually a lot worse than that. He is on crutches, has to go through physical therapy, face is a little swollen, and he is supposed to have somebody home to take care of him. He might, which is probably the reason he turned down my help, but definitely worse than a cold.”

“Did he say how he ended up there?” she asked.

Grabbing the remote off the nightstand, he walked around to his side of the bed, pulled his daughter into his arms, and scrolled to find him and her a movie to watch.

“Did you hear me?”

“My bad, naw he didn’t,” he lied and said.

“Oh okay, well that was a lot, but I’m glad you got to help him and you guys got to talk. That’s big and should take some of that weight off you’ve been carrying about the situation.”

Shocked at her words and no further pursuit of inquiring about the situation had Tarven smiling from ear to ear. He started to feel like he had truly won, and his assumption that he would lose her was wrong. The love of his life was not rushing out the door to hunt down the man she was willing to risk everything and everybody for had him floating on a cloud. And more in love than ever before.

What he did not know is that the love of his life had learned to not show her hand as did before. She had to be a lot more careful than all the other times and act accordingly.

CHAPTER 12

After dinner was had from their favorite chicken wing spot, they had a movie night in the living room watching Kaleigh's favorite movie Trolls for the hundredth time. Tarven took Kaleigh into her bedroom to put her in bed as Ginger had fallen asleep on the couch.

With Tarven ready for bed himself, he went and kissed Ginger on the forehead and told her he was going to bed. She had awakened and said she would be coming to bed soon, but needed to go over some charts for work first.

No reason to doubt her, he went on and as soon as his head hit the pillow he was out. The problem that he left untouched was the thought that Ginger had heard all she wanted and was satisfied.

The minute she saw Tarven lay across the bed, she knew he would be out. As he went down, she waited about ten minutes before she stood up and did a quick run around the couch. Mixed in with a silent scream of joy to know that Keiontay was back in town. She knew she had to find a way to see him somehow.

"I will suck that man's soul out if I get the chance, but I have to play it cool. I just need to see him one last time," she thought to herself as she pulled out her laptop to access Tarven's phone.

SInce the last time she had to guess Keiontay's password, she had found out on social media that there was an app that gave her access to a person's phone if she paid the right price. She was willing to pay whatever to find out what she needed to know. She tried it on Keiontay but realized he changed his number. So about the time she had learned about it, it was no good, but with the latest information from Tarven, it came just on time.

She logged into the site, entered Tarven's phone number and like the red carpet the files and apps she wanted to pry through rolled out on the screen. With her eyes big with excitement she hoped she could find what she was looking for before he got up. Because checking on her in the middle of the night when she stayed up after him is something he always did. So she knew she had to move fast.

"I wonder if that bitch Nova knows where he is or has she been seeing him?" she thought to herself as she scrolled. "I will focus on that later, for now, I just need to find his ride log for today and get the last address listed. Then boom that will get me a little closer to seeing my man."

As she scrolled through the rideshare log, she watched the door and listened for movement. Her heart was pounding through her chest as she hoped her snooping would go by fast. "He said he took him home, I wonder what area he moved to? I'm proud of him though to get back on his feet. I know Tarven is exaggerating about what we did fucking him up. That man is a soldier inside and out. He's used to my bullshit, so that was no sweat off his nose. Maybe a little gut punch, but he's fine. Tarven just wanted me to feel bad," she said to herself as she continued to scroll and reached the bottom of the ride log.

She smiled as her eyes grew large looking at the address staring back at her, but noticed that it had been labeled as canceled . Hopefully it was the same address he ended up taking him to. She copied and pasted the address into the web search engine to see how far he was from her, and hoped that she started out on the right trail. She wanted to look at the log a little longer, but saw Tarven sit up on the side of the bed and instantly closed the laptop out of fear he would catch her.

"You still out here?," he asked as he came out of the room rubbing his eyes looking at her.

"Yeah, still kind of energized so I was just going to focus on some work for work tomorrow," she stated as she looked at him.

"Well beautiful you can finish working. I will just sit here next to you and watch a few highlights until I get back sleepy," he said as he reached for the remote.

"No," she blurted out, startling him.

"Damn, girl you scared me, but what do you mean no?"

"No, you shouldn't watch tv out here because if you fall asleep then you won't be next to me in the bed when I get done. I would have to sleep without you. I don't want that," she explained.

"Makes sense cause it probably won't take long before I'm back out again. At least I will feel you when you get in bed."

"Exactly," she said smiling.

Leaning down to give her a kiss, "don't stay up too long," he said and put down the remote and headed back to the bedroom.

"Whew," she said as she saw him lay back in bed and turn the tv on. She opened her laptop back and saw that the address was not far from her. The satellite map showing the pin of a hotel made her feel confused.

"Did he get dropped off at the hotel, live near it, or maybe met somebody there? Like damn, if I ask Tarven about Keiontay, I will give myself away that I'm still interested. I see that he feels so much better to think Keiontay is someone he doesn't have to worry about anymore, and I don't want to ruin that for him. So I have to use my own skills of investigation," she thought to herself.

Before she got up to head to the bedroom, she went into the history tab and cleared what she had been doing to not leave behind any evidence. Headed to bed with a smile in her heart and feeling like she was about to be back in the game of juggling the love of her life and the man she desired, she was more than ready for sunrise to come.

"DId you get everything finished?" Tarven asked as she sat on the bed.

"I thought you were asleep," she responded.

"A little, but I felt you sit up on the side of the bed," he said.

"Ah okay, but before you go to sleep mister man, let's discuss how I'm going to get to work in the morning with all my windows missing?" she asked as she looked at him. He turned over to look at her and started laughing.

"Ah damn you put that pussy on me so good, I had forgotten," he said and laughed. " Plus it's like now you got the clearest views and best breeze from all angles.

"Ha ha ha, very funny! Your little attitude outburst was cute, but I have to work tomorrow. I know you're going to work, and Kaleigh has to go to daycare, so a solution is needed."

"All of that is true, but you're saying all that like the car no longer works, the windows are just gone," he said and smiled.

"You think this shit funny huh?" she asked.

"A little," he admitted.

"Tarven, I am not going to drive to work with all my windows busted. Like the amount of questions that would come at me, I do not need that. Everybody won't understand our level of love and crazy. Plus I don't want people in my business."

"Aw, you're embarrassed," he mocked.

"Tarven! I'm serious!"

"I'm just messing with you baby! I mean I can switch my schedule to work evenings, or I can drop you off at work. No big deal really, and most of the time I am the one picking up Kaleigh in the afternoon anyway. So I don't see the big problem."

"But what about when I need lunch, have to go to meetings, and have to make certain trips for the office."

"Ginger, you act like I can't come and do those things for you just the same. Plus it's not like you're going to rent a car or something, that would be a waste of money."

"Tarven, I know you will be more than ready to do everything I need and I appreciate that so much, but I do not work as hard as I do to depend on someone."

"But you're depending on me, which is a part of partnership and a relationship. Being there for one another is a part of being us. Plus it shouldn't take that long to get your windows replaced."

"Tarven, if you haven't realized it, but we're not rich and that is just money out the window that we need. So it's probably going to take some time to get them all fixed."

"Ginger, stop that lying girl. I know we don't fully disclose our financial situation to each other, but you are a money hoarder baby!"

"Yeah, for emergencies and savings."

"Well, if you don't consider this an emergency then so be it, I can't force you. What do you think I should pay for it? Is that what you're hinting at?"

"I mean no, but since you brought it up, to at least pay for half I would surely appreciate it!"

"Okay, cool, give me until the middle of next week and I got you. Call and get some quotes and whatever the quote be, I will do half. Does that work for you?"

"It does, but what to do in the meantime?" she said out loud until it hit her, "that's it!" she said out loud starling Tarven.

"What did you decide?" he asked.

Not wanting to divulge her plans in mind she just shared that she was going to rent a car.

"With me renting a car, I can do my handy work without worrying about Tarven seeing me because it won't be my car. And Keiontay for sure won't know who I am," she thought to herself and started smiling.

Noticing Ginger's smile, "I'm glad that makes you happy now let's go to bed so we can be rested for tomorrow. You know Kaleigh is going to get up with enough energy for ten people," he said and started to laugh as he laid down.

With a smile still planted on her face, she said he was more than right and turned out the light. She was going to sleep feeling like the life she was missing a great part of for a little over a year, she stood a chance of finally getting back.

As the sun rose and the day came in, the two awakened with much to achieve in their day. The only difference is, what Ginger had in mind was something Tarven had no clue about.

The plan was to drop Kaleigh off at daycare, take Ginger to go get a rental car so she could get back and forth to work until her windows were replaced, and then he would start his shift. To Tarven that was the exact plan. For Ginger, once Kaleigh was dropped off and she got to the rental car place, she had an alternate plan mapped out.

He offered to wait with her but she declined as she knew he could spoil the timing of her plans she configured. So to not draw any attention to herself, she pretended that she was concerned about him getting in as many hours as he could. When in reality, she really just wanted him gone. It limited the chances of him following her at any point or noticing that she wasn't going directly to work today.

Once they finished all the paperwork thirty five minutes later, she was now driving a black Dodge Challenger. For her, this was perfect and something no one would ever expect her to be in. Before driving off the lot, she called her office and told them that she had run into a family issue and would not be in until after 1pm that day. As well as that any appointments scheduled for today could be moved to later or the next day. She was okay with playing catch up for the chance to see the man she had been missing miserably.

With the office informed, car rented, and address pulled up, she was more than ready to do some exploring to connect some dots that would hopefully lead her to Keiontay. She drove until she reached the hotel, and thought about boldly going inside and asking for his room number. However, she knew that wouldn't work because she couldn't risk him seeing her.

"If he sees me or sees me coming, I stand a chance of him going in another direction or avoiding me. I have to just wait this out," she thought to herself as she circled the parking lot twice trying to decide where she should park to get the best view.

"But if he's not feeling well, there's a chance he won't be coming out, but he's too stubborn to just lay in the bed all day like he's supposed to. I can only imagine how miserable he must be," she said to herself as she finally parked on the back of the hotel. She decided to wait there until about 12:30pm and then would switch to the front side the next day. Her goal for the week was to try a side a day until she got a chance to see him.

What she would say is something she had not thought of yet. Hopefully whatever she said wouldn't sound too crazy and it would be believable. For the first three days it was just people going in and out and her watching her surroundings. She revisited the idea of asking for a key to his room and surprise him, but with him not being in the best condition she didn't want to risk upsetting him.

Over the course of her stake out, Tarven believed she was at work. Her job was under the assumption that she was dealing with personal family matters, as to why her schedule was now so uncertain as opposed to her usual concrete appointments that she never strayed from. About time she would finish her observation for the day she would head back to the office and take on her patients as though nothing happened. She was doing everything like usual and nobody suspected a thing until Ginger's what had become a normal gloomy face had turned into a smile. She was smiling more than ever and it could be told that something new had to be going on in her life. She was more cheerful at work and letting dental assistants slide with certain things that she normally had not. The staff was loving this new side of her. While Tarven saw her finally seeing the happiness in their relationship and enjoying the idea of their little family.

She had them all fooled. Though she had not seen Keiontay yet, the thought that she was in the same place as he laid his head, and the possibility of her seeing him soon had her in better spirits than she had been in months. The part of her she thought had died was coming back to life and that made her happier as the anticipation built.

****

On the day that Tarven had dropped him off, shit was hitting the fan that he needed to get his shit together and soon. Getting that call from Malachi had him on edge of either playing it safe or risking it all. With not being able to walk fully on his own the thought to risk it all definitely fell to the bottom of the list every time he weighed his options.

Morgan had kept her word that day and had come to check on him which was a great help because his assumption that he could do it on his own was wrong. And though the whole ordeal seemed crazy, he had no choice plus he saw it as a fresh start almost. On the second day that Morgan came over when she got off work is when Keiontay put the ball in her court, in hopes that she could be just as crazy as him and take a chance.

Once she came into the room with Wendy's in hand, he smiled, and said, "it's like you read my mind".

"Or I know your butt been in this room all day and hungry as hell," she laughed as she handed him his food.

Smiling as he looked in the bag and saw two burgers, fries, and chicken nuggets with two different types of sauces. Assuming that the other stuff was for her, he reached in the bag and picked out what he wanted or thought was his and tried to hand her back the bag.

"Oh no, that's all yours," she said. "I bought you extras so you can have something for later. Plus I ate a salad from Zaxby's a little before I got off," she said.

"Aren't you sweet," he said as she sat on the edge of the bed.

"I guess, so how is your pain level today?" she asked.

"It's manageable for the most part as long as I don't move much. But before I get into knowing how your day went, I kind of want to get into something important that I need to run past you."

"Okay," she said as she looked at him with concern in her eyes.

"Um, well, I won't go into full detail about it, but I decided to pay somebody back that I owe. It hasn't left me with not much money to continue to stay here plus with buying food etc, and with me not being able to work right now, I'm kind of in a tough spot. What I have left from paying the person I owe, if I continue to stay here, I will be out on my ass probably by Saturday without a dime left to my name. I can't get a place without me working at the moment, and family wise I'm not trying to go back home to my folks and be paraded with questions."

"Ah, wow," she said as she stood to her feet and looked at him.

Unsure of what she was about to say or do, he said nothing as he waited for her to speak.

"Wow, umm that's a lot and that's definitely asking a lot, but shit'd you asking me that is no stranger than me volunteering to help you with taking care of your bandages and bringing you food. I guess we are both crazy as hell," she said and started laughing.

"From the looks of it, shit kind of crazy, but hell there's people that get married to people they've never even met before," he said. Laughing slightly, "you're right, that's actually one of my favorite shows to be honest," she admitted.

"So, what are you saying?" he asked.

"Assuming that's what you're hinting at, yes Keiontay Clark, you can move in with me," she said and smiled.

"Are you serious?" he asked.

"I mean, it's not like I am at home much with the way my shifts go sometimes. I don't have any kids, not expecting, not dating really, no dogs or cats even, just me. I have a few friends that might come over here and there, but otherwise than that, it's usually just me."

"So you're all about making your coins huh?" he inquired.

"Umm, the money is okay, but I truly just enjoy helping people. I'm sure it sounds corny, but it's just always been a dream of mine to help in my community. Working in the medical field was like the gateway for me to do so," she expressed.

"Aw, how Ms. I Desire-World-Peace of you," he said and started laughing.

"Ha ha ha, very funny, it kind of sounds like that ordeal but that's really just me!"

"I'm just messing with you. I feel that though, it takes a lot of heart to be selfless like that," he said.

"I guess, never put too much thought into it, but umm before fully agreeing to you moving in, I want to be transparent with you," she started to say.

"Ah hell, let me guess, you got a crazy ass ex boyfriend?"

"You're funny, but no. In a month or so, I'm moving to Dallas, Texas for a new job so you wouldn't have much time to get yourself together, that's all," she explained. "I just wanted to tell you ahead of time so that you could factor that into your equation."

"You said that like that was a bad thing."

"It's not a bad thing, but I just don't think seven weeks is a lot of time to get your life together. If that was so, the whole world would have their shit together," she stated.

"Well, since you're crazy and I am too, would it be so crazy if I moved to Dallas too? I need a new start actually and once I got my strength back fully I was leaving anyway."

"Oh boy, this is crazy! I feel like a camera crew should be standing to the side recording all this because this is insane. I have to be borderline insane myself cause, why not?" she said, humping her shoulders.

"Yeah we are both crazy, but I guess in seven weeks, we will learn a lot about each other."

"So you'll go to Dallas with me for real?" she asked.

"I mean if you'll have me is the thing. I don't want to impose more than I already am!"

"Truthfully, I was nervous about moving to another state alone and been praying on what to do, and have even considered not going. So maybe this is my answer I have been praying for, I don't know but I'm going to take this as a positive sign." she stated as she started looking around his room.

"What are you looking at?" he asked, noticing her looking around.

"Trying to see how much stuff you have and trying to determine how long it will take to pack it all."

"Man I can't believe you're being this good to me, some has to be wrong that you're not telling," he said and started laughing. "Your family takes in patients and experiments on them or some? Make them work for them or some?"

"Hell, I can say the same, what, you meet females, kill them and hide their bodies?" she said looking at him.

"True dat, true dat, naw, just in a man trying to pull himself up by the bootstraps," he said.

"I hear you, so, pack tonight and move out tomorrow into my place? Or how much longer until you have to check out?"

"I pay for a week at a time, so it would be the end of the week for my check out time, but I would much rather get the hell on as soon as possible!"

CHAPTER 13

On the third day of observation she changed up her times and decided to go after work instead. Hoping that maybe her change of times would get her some different results. Plus it got the office off her back from asking about the so-called issues she was having. She headed back to the hotel after she got off work and parked on the back. She said to herself that if this stake out didn't work, she would ask for one of her doctor friends to access some medical records for her to see when he was originally discharged.

The back up plan was to be in the parking lot of his follow up appointment when and wherever that was in order to see him. She was determined to see him and had the hopes that things would go back to her normal of having her cake and eating it too. Her promise to herself was that if she got him back this time that she would do better, respect his boundaries, and wouldn't cross the line.

As she sat in her rental car, between scrolling through her phone and watching the door, her eyes looked up at a point and became fixated on this girl that could be Ryan Destiny's twin. Her melanin was a beautiful brown hue, shoulder length straight black hair, about 5'5 and had an hourglass shape that was wearing scrubs.

"I'm sure people go to work from here just like anybody else, but I don't know," Ginger said to herself as she felt herself drawn to the girl and watched her every move.

At first she came down and put a suitcase and a few bags in a white and black jeep renegade and then went back inside. It just appeared that whoever she was checking out. She didn't think too much of it until she looked up from her phone a second to see her carrying a hospital discharge bag along with a duffle bag.

"Now that is something," Ginger said as she sat up and put her phone down to get a better view of what she was looking at. "I don't want to jump to conclusions, maybe she's a nurse that was sick...or maybe she was sent to come check on him and move him out. He must be worse than what Tarven said. Maybe they're moving him to a facility or something," she continued to guess as she looked on before further speculating.

"Maybe I should just kindly go up to her and ask what she's doing here?" Ginger thought. "But that might be too much and I don't want to blow my cover," she continued to think as she watched the female go back inside. Ginger continued to watch the door more eagerly than ever now.

About fifteen minutes passed and she had not come back down. Ginger had mustered the nerve to go wait by the door and make it seem like she was a guest that had left her room key. Then she would bump into her and make some small talk in hopes that she could answer her assumptions. However, as she was about to get out of the car, the door opened and Ginger quickly closed her door back, unsure if it was her or someone else. As she put her attention on the door, her mouth dropped as her waiting had finally paid off. A guy on some crutches with some Nike joggers and t-shirt was taking his time coming out. She wanted to jump out of her skin as the excitement consumed her body. She wanted to scream because crutches or not she recognized that face and her heart was beating fast with excitement and nervousness.

"Oh my God! It's him!" she said out loud and slid down in her seat as her outburst had caused them to stop and look around. Not sure in which direction the voice came from, they frantically looked around, but saw nothing, brushed it off and just kept moving.

As they made it to her jeep, she opened the passenger door and helped him in and put his crutches in the back seat. As he closed his door, she went back in and Keiontay was left alone in the car.

Ginger figured that now would be perfect, but how to explain her being there was something she had not figured out. She knew that if he discovered that she had been there watching him, they would already be off to a bad start and she didn't want that. So she decided to continue her surveillance and follow them to where they were headed.

About five minutes later, the female came back down with one last bag, put it in the car, got in the car, and began to pull out of the parking space.

Ginger hit the steering wheel with frustration as she watched them drive away a little before she crunk up her car to follow them. "Ginger, what are you doing?" she asked herself as she trailed the car but stayed far enough behind to try not to be seen. "Maybe I should just go home," she thought to herself as continued to follow behind the jeep and two cars until her phone rang and startled her.

Answering her phone without looking, "Hello", she said.

“Babe, where are you?” Tarven asked startling her more because her normal one hour observation she had been doing since she started had gone over into almost three hours.

Trying to think quickly on her feet, but still buy her enough time to continue following them to their destination so she wouldn’t lose her lead she said, “Hey baby, I forgot to call you and let you know. One of the dentists from across town contacted me and asked if I could come by and check out some x-rays they had done on a patient. We started talking and lost track of time. I should be home in a little bit, is everything okay?”

“You could’ve shot me a text or some because I was a little worried. Plus it's almost time for dinner and I wanted to see if you wanted me to cook or if I should order something for tonight,” he stated.

“Ah, umm that’s sweet,” she started to say before she became the car behind them instead of two cars behind. “Oh shit, shit!” she said as she reduced her speed and got behind another car.

“Is everything okay?” Tarven asked.

“Huh?” Ginger asked, forgetting that Tarven was on the phone still.

“I was asking were you okay. I heard you saying oh shit.”

"Oh, my bad, yeah my bad, somebody had swerved in my lane and I didn't see them, but babe, let me go so I can concentrate on this road. These people are crazy."

"I thought you were with your colleague. How are you driving?"

"I just told you that I was headed home Tarven. In fact, I'll grab something to eat for us on my way in," she suggested.

"No, you didn't but it's cool. What's done in the dark will come to the light."

"Don't fucking start Tarven!"

"I'm not Ginger! I'll get Kaleigh and I something to eat. You just worry about you and whatever you're doing," he said and ended the call.

Shaking her head at Tarven's phone call, she made her way back to two cars behind Keiontay. About thirty minutes later, they arrived at some apartments that sat down in a valley. When the two cars in front of her turned off before them, she still waited before turning into the complex. Ginger kept her distance as there weren't many places to park where she wouldn't be noticed or suspicious.

As they parked into a parking space that was almost directly in front of an apartment, she continued to drive down the hill closer to the river near the apartment complex. She backed in, parked, and had the best view of Keiontay and the female.

******

"Please don't tell me you stay on the top floor," he said as he looked at the two flights of steps that zigzagged to the top apartments.

As she took the key out of the ignition, she started laughing and said, "we're going to just have to take our time I guess."

"Take our time! Hell naw that's not even fair to you and me on these crutches plus steps, I don't trust myself," he started to explain.

Before he could go on, "relax," she said with a smile on her face. "I stay on the bottom apartment actually, so chill. No biggie. I'll help you in and then I'll get your stuff out."

"I feel so bad," he said..

"Why?" she asked as she began to open the car door.

"Because I can't help you. I feel like I'm putting everything on you and that doesn't feel fair. Like mentally it's fucking with me on so many levels," he explained.

"I get it, but I'm sure if you could do for yourself or even help me you would, and we would have probably never met actually. You seem pretty strong willed. Whatever you were doing before you were holding it down for yourself, you just ran into a snag. It happens to the best of us."

"Man you hell!" he said and started laughing.

"Far from it! Probably the most peace you've ever come across," she said and got out of the car and came around to his side of the car.

As Ginger watched in the distance without them knowing, Morgan helped Keiontay inside her apartment and then began to carry his stuff inside her apartment. Once they got in, she sat his stuff to the side, handed him the remote off of her coffee table and headed to her closet to change out of her work clothes.

"So how long have you been here?" he asked as he scrolled through the TV guide.

"Ummm, like almost three years, but I'm glad to be moving soon. Though it's just me, I want more room and not have everything in one spot," she said as she came out of the closet in some Nike biker shorts with a matching crop top.

"Damn," he said as he looked up at her when she came out of the closet back into the living area.

"What?" she asked as she sat Indian style on the sofa next to him and started to scroll through her phone.

"It's my first time seeing you outside of your scrubs, didn't know you had a body like that under there I guess."

"Oh, these are my chill, off work clothes where I just want to be comfy."

"So you just bring strangers to your home often huh? Cause you are so chill about this shit."

She started laughing and it startled him slightly, "ah hell, I knew it," he said.

Waving her hand as she tried to stop laughing, "I'm laughing cause I told myself that you were probably thinking I do shit like this all the time, but I truly don't. You are the first. Then I was like what is the most he could do to me when he can barely walk? Swing on me with one of your crutches that I could just easily grab," she said and started back laughing.

"Well damn! You don't have to do me like that," he said and started laughing.

"I'm sorry, but I just have to keep it real with you. I was thinking shit out in my head for my own safety. I can have a good heart, but I don't have to put myself in the crossfire of danger. Maybe not the smartest thing to do or anything I will probably ever do again, cause it's kind of reckless, but so far so good hopefully."

Keiontay started laughing as he looked at her and shook his head, and then put his attention back on the tv until she broke the silence in the room.

"Umm, so what's your story Mr. Clark? What's the real tea?" she said as she turned to face him.

"I figured this would come up sooner than later so I might as well go ahead and get it over with now. I'll give the short version. I had reached a point in my life where I felt like I had finally made it! I had finally graduated from the ghetto and reckless lifestyle I was once used to. I let go of a toxic ass ex, got my own place, was working a good ass job, and was saving for my dream car. Speaking of, I need to call around and figure out where my car is, but any who...I was saving for my car and as I was enjoying life. I got hit with a curve ball that my ex was pregnant. I wanted to do right by my child, but that didn't mean we had to be together."

"Right," she said, agreeing with him before he continued.

"So that's what I tried to do, but she wanted it her or no way at all. I gave her space and started back dating. Then I met who I feel like was the love of my life and I fucked it up repeatedly. Didn't protect her enough, didn't stand up for her, probably left her at the worst time when she needed me, and when she took me back despite my fuck ups, I still fucked up. I saw my errors and was disappointed in myself and wanted to just run away from it all. She told me to just get my shit together and give her time to heal, but I wasn't trying to hear that. Felt like she wasn't hearing what I thought was right, so I dipped. Got mixed back in the reckless shit I once prayed to get out of, shortened the wrong person, and my current state is the result of my bad decisions."

"Wow! That's a lot and if that's the short version, the details must be crazy."

Keiontay said nothing as a part of him felt exposed.

"I mean honestly, from listening to it all, it sounds like you made a lot of choices from not healing from those traumas you endured early on. I once heard that if you don't heal from pain, you continue to carry it with you and it leads you to picking or making some bad decisions. Then the girl you feel like was the love of your life, she was ready to love you as you are, but you weren't ready for her because of things you've been through. That's no excuse, but you couldn't see her greatness until now because you were standing in front of your own self. Disqualifying yourself without even giving yourself a chance. Basically sabotaging stuff before it could form into something that could hurt you. I don't know your full story, but it's giving that there was somebody that failed to show up for you. So when you found a person that truly made you happy, the blank space of how to show up for somebody you love became a phase you shut out or run from because that's what you're used to. But making the decision to finally work on you shows a great bit of growth. The best form of growth is being able to communicate that you're working on healing and your overall self. Instead of just up and leaving. That absence of the unknown then creates that why am I not good enough, what did I do wrong type of questions, and that's unfair to that person. Because you now give them a part of your pain you were carrying, that I'm sure they don't want.

Keiontay turned his head away from her as her words resonated throughout his head, and a single tear fell from his eye.

"I feel like you keep thinking you're this bad person because of the mistakes you've made not realizing that you're human and still growing. You just suck at communicating."

Wiping his hand across his face to not make it noticeable of the tear that had fell, he started to laugh, "I definitely suck at communicating."

"Most guys do," she said and started to smile. "Just don't give up on you and those you love. If you love her and truly feel she's the love of your life, get you together, and then reach back out, but be willing to be patient and understanding. Especially knowing that you just up and dipped out on her. If she talks to you she's going to have a million questions, and need reassurance fifty million times and one.

"You seem wise for a young cat. How old are you again?"

"I thought I told you already but twenty seven."

"Not too young, but definitely got some wisdom on you I see."

"You live and you learn."

"True that! So what's your story? Why are you single, living here alone?"

"A few too many bad relationships. Then once I decided I was moving to another state I figured what was the point. Plus, I wanted to stay focused on my career."

"Well that was short and to the point. I should've told my story like that," he said.

"You could have, but you didn't. It's okay, I enjoyed listening to you."

"How sweet," he said, cracking a smile before continuing. "But to circle back, what do you define as bad relationships?"

"To each's own, but for me bad was dating someone that verbally abused me every chance he got. He made me feel like I was shit at the bottom of a barrel. He covered it up so well when it came to us being around people that it used to fuck with my mind. His words were so smooth that it was like he was stabbing me while hiding the blood. So three years too long I stayed. Then there was a short term relationship I endured. He was full of love, helped heal me, but he was stagnant, damn near refusing to grow. The most recent one, I thought he was my one. Everything about him was damn near perfect, but he insisted that we have a poly relationship and I wasn't with that, so I had to walk away. Made me feel like just me wasn't enough even though he claimed I was. So yeah one too many bad relationships like I said."

"Wow! Thank you for not letting me feel like I was the only one between us that been through some pretty fucked up shit early on in life."

"You're welcome," she said as they both burst into laughter.

"Life is truly crazy as hell at times. But before we get deeper into who each other, can we order some food? My stomach is touching my back right now."

Shaking her head, yeah we can but I much rather just go and grab it. I'm frugal. I would prefer to save from them high ass delivery fees.

"You right," he said and started laughing. "But dinner on me."

"I'm not arguing with you there, what do you want?"

"Chinese food?"

"That can work, an eggroll and egg drop soup sounds good right about now."

"Definitely not what I will be getting, but I hear you."

"What do you want then?" she asked as she began to start putting on her shoes, grabbing her phone and keys.

"It's weird I think, but I like to order enough food so that I can snack on it in the middle of the night. Like it takes out the thought of figuring out what to eat in a sense. And to me, Chinese food after it's reheated seems like it takes the food to another level."

Laughing at him slightly, "Okay, I hear you. If you say so, but you still haven't told me what you are getting."

"Ah damn...chicken fried rice, general tso chicken, and crab puffs if they have them depending on the restaurant."

"That's a lot."

"See, but it's like for now and later."

"You act like you're not going to eat tomorrow."

"Man don't do that, I just told you my deal."

"I know, I'm just messing with you. So do you want to just cashapp me the money or is it going to be cash, or card?"

"Oh, you thought I wasn't going? I understand."

"I did. I figured you would just want to rest and get settled in a little more."

"Umm naw, plus I want to see what Chinese spots are around here. Can't just be going to any of them because some of that shit just tastes like cardboard or it's microwaved."

"I hear you, well let's hop to it before stuff starts closing."

Hours had gone by and Ginger was still posted outside. Since she knew where he would be, she decided to go ahead and leave before she had to think of a lie grand enough to cover up how she had spent most of her day. On the way out, she decided that she would get the girl's license plate number to find out a little about who she was.

Focused on getting the license plate number, her focus fell from her surroundings. As she pulled behind the car to take a picture of the license plate, her phone died as soon she snapped the picture. Trying to quickly find her charger to see if she captured the picture, or if she needed to take another one, she quickly grew impatient. She started to look in her glove compartment and console for a pen or something she could write it down on instead. Filled with frustration and trying to move fast, she missed her opportunity as the door of the apartment opened. The mysterious girl was now in the door frame with Keiontay behind her.

Ginger took her foot off the brake, and drove off. She prayed that neither one of them had a chance to look inside the car.

“Did you see that?” Morgan asked as she looked at Keiontay as they came out of the door and locked it.

“Probably just somebody looking for an apartment or making a delivery, wrong address, leaving out, the possibilities are endless,” he said.

“But I’ve never seen a dodge challenger over here.”

Keiontay humped his shoulders and made his way to the car, and she followed behind him to help him in the car.

“It just doesn’t make any sense to me, especially for them to leave the minute we opened the door.”

“I hear you, but I wouldn’t think anything of it,” he said. He looked at his phone and thought to himself that it could have possibly had something to do with him. However, giving it further attention was something he wasn’t doing. Because staying with her and getting to move to another state was like an upgrade in his plan, and he was not about to mess that up.

CHAPTER 14

As they drove to the restaurant, music played and they made small talk, but Keiontay's mind was truly somewhere else.

"Everything in me just tells me that it had something to do with me, and I hate that shit. It was either Ginger or somebody associated with Malachi. I sent Malachi his money through cashapp, but he didn't respond. We should be good, hopefully. Then with me coming in contact with Tarven, I knew he ain't keep his mouth shut cause he probably think he doesn't have anything to worry about. Probably thinking he den won her for real, not knowing that Ginger is like a possum. She knows how to play the part when necessary," he thought to himself as he scrolled through his phone.

"You okay?" she asked as they arrived at the first restaurant.

"Yeah, just thinking about some stuff," he said as he looked up. "I don't like this spot, can we go to the one on Briarcliff instead."

"That's not too far from here. That's cool."

They placed their orders, waited, and took the food back to the apartment to eat. It was like they were old friends catching up. It was an odd comfortability between the both of them. However, on the other end of town was Ginger, headed home frustrated that she almost got caught. And now she had to deal with Tarven.

As soon as she walked in, Tarven was sitting in the living room reading Kaleigh a bedtime story. Noticing she was nodding off as he read, she walked lightly to the bedroom and laid across the bed as she was filled with so many emotions. Plus it felt good to stretch out after sitting in that car for so long.

About fifteen to twenty minutes later, Tarven went to lay down a sleeping Kaleigh in her room. Then shortly after went into the bedroom with Ginger and sat at the bottom of the bed.

"Ginger, I love you and I have been patient with you time after time, so please save me the bullshit. What were you really out doing? Because you and I both know you weren't looking at no damn x-rays for this long. Nor did it take you from whatever you were that long to get home."

Ginger had yet to think of a lie. So she remained silent as she thought about just coming clean and telling him the truth.

"I know you heard me. Just tell me. Are you talking to somebody else? I'm tired of coming second in your life when it comes to love. Let me know now."

Sitting up and deciding to just skate her way through it because she truly didn't want to lose Tarven, she decided to lie. "Babe, no, you're going to ruin it but I won't give you the full details. I can see how it looks a little fishy. But I was out putting some stuff together for you. I don't have much time in the day with work, so I just decided to go when I got off to make sure it all come together."

"Working on what Ginger?"

"Babe, it's a surprise. Just something to show you how much I appreciate you for being the man you are to me and the father you've been to our daughter."

"That sounds sweet and all, but I still smell bullshit in the midst"

Leaning over and hugging him around his neck, "you'll see, you're going to love it when everything is ready."

"Sure," he said and took her arms from around him and stood up. "I'm about to go take a shower. I had bought you a piece of your favorite cake while we were out. It's in the fridge."

"Thank you for thinking about me, but I would much rather take a shower with you first," she said as she stood up and started taking her clothes off and walking towards him.

****

Nova was still trying to process Omar's now aggressive and assertive behavior that she used to dream about from the minute she realized she wanted more than just sex from him. The days she used to crave him spending the night, holding her, them laughing, talking, and just enjoying each other's company was like a fantasy world for her. But now that it was a reality, she was having a hard time wrapping her head around everything. She wanted to dive head first into love with Omar. Live out every dream she ever imagined, but she was restrained with hesitation.

She didn't want to place doubt in the situation, but she asked herself why now? What had changed. He had answered those questions, but felt like it was more he possibly was not saying. From the moment he left her that day in the parking lot of her apartment, he was revealing to be the man she always believed he could be. When she got off work, he would have dinner ready at his place for her and Nolan, or send money for dinner on the days he was working and couldn't stop by. He had started sending her floral arrangements and taking her on dates that she used to tell him she wanted to do, but never thought he was listening. Then the icing on the cake, when it came to Nolan's first birthday that she was at first stressing about, he helped her pull it off and showed up bearing gifts.

With the time ticking away and the more time spent together, she was working her way into that honeymoon phase. Where she was picturing what life could be for the two of them. After all, she wasn't getting any younger and to finally be with someone she desired initially, she was leaning towards finally living her dream come true.

But in the back of her mind, she was wondering what that other shoe was going to be when it dropped.

Despite her doubts of the what ifs she was enjoying the chance of smiling again, feeling safe, like someone was finally there consistently for her and Nolan, and she didn't have to look over her shoulder.

While reaching the final stretch of another shift at the pharmacy, one of Nova's co-workers noticed she was staring at her phone. She had a big grin on her face as she worked on getting the prescriptions finished for the day.

"Must be a pretty good text message to have you smiling like that," she said, catching Nova's attention.

"Huh?" she said, trying to understand what she was talking about.

"You've been doing this a little bit longer than me, and I know first hand that after a while all these damn pills start looking the same. So whatever or shall I say whoever it is, has you over there smiling like it's payday and your check just deposited," she said and started laughing.

Putting a label on the two twenty dram prescriptions, placing them in the basket to be checked and bagged, Nova looked at her co-worker and smiled from ear to ear.

"Oh my God! Girl, it's just a guy friend of mine. It's nothing. He was just being silly and it had me laughing inside thinking about it," Nova said.

"Girl, when I first started talking to my boyfriend, you were me. Everything that man did had me smiling from ear to ear. I'm not trying to get in your business, but if your friend got you smiling like that, you might need to reconsider that title. Because in the time you have worked here, I have never seen you smile so much. Not even being funny, but when you were pregnant you seemed stressed out a lot. There was some excitement and smiles, but nothing like this," her co-worker explained before the bell went off signaling that a customer was at the counter.

As her co-worker walked away, Nova quickly fell into a daze as she replayed her words in her head.

"I was happy with Keiontay, it's just when all the shit started hitting the fan, it was at times hard to be as happy as I wanted. With never knowing what headache was going to unfold, it was a lot. With Omar there's no drama, so maybe that's why I smile a little more.

Are we just friends? I know he wanted to be more serious and has been showing he's serious, but is his serious the same as mine. I think it's best I ask before things get any further, but a part of me doesn't want to bring it up. I feel like I shouldn't have to, ugh I hate dating," Nova thought as she started pulling leaflets off of the printer to pull medications.

Ready to finish her shift, pick up Nolan, and head home she put her phone in her pocket and paid it no further mind. Her only concern about her phone was if it rang because it could be pertaining to her son, but all else could wait.

Once she clocked out and went to grab her belongings out of her locker, she took her phone out of her pocket and was shocked to see the multiple text messages from Omar. It was like the time he texted her was around the time she was thinking about him. She felt like he must have had to be thinking about her too, or it was a strange coincidence.

Omar: Hey beautiful, I hope you're having a good day today. I wanted to know if we could meet for dinner tonight?

Omar: If the answer will be yes, I have reservations for us, and I will shoot you the time and address. Or I can come and pick you guys up.

Omar: Just let me know when you get a chance. I hope I get to see you today.

As she read his text messages, she got chills all over her body and felt like she wanted to melt into the floor. Closing her locker and putting her airpods in, she called him, and headed for her car.

He answered on the second ring, and her face lit up like Times Square during New Years Eve.

"Did you get my message?" he asked before she could say hello.

Laughing slightly, "well dang give me a minute to get in the car," she said as she put her purse in the passenger seat and closed the door.

"My bad, let me backup. Hey, how was your day?" he asked as he heard her crank up the car.

"It was decent. Nothing too rough. A little distracted here and there, but I pulled through."

"Humph, was thinking about me huh? It's okay cause I was thinking about you too."

"Oh were you?"

"Yes, which is why I made plans for us tonight. I would love to get an answer back if you're able to give me one at the moment.

She hesitated as she debated if she should bring her questions up now or push them off, but decided to go with putting them off. Maybe face to face would definitely be better.

"Yes Omar," she said as she smiled and made it to Nolan's daycare.

"Yes!" he screamed!

"You're silly man! You act like it's that deep. What if I had said no?"

"I can't lie I would've been disappointed and probably have asked the captain if I could have picked up another shift."

"Really? Why not just go home?" she inquired as she began to get out of the car.

"Sometimes, I just don't like to be alone or feel like I'm doing nothing."

"So is that how you found your way back to me because you were bored?" she asked as she went inside to get Nolan.

"Because I don't like being alone doesn't mean I was lonely. Not as in I was talking to someone, but as in no. No I am not talking to you cause I'm bored. I know it's going to take some reassurance with the way I moved initially and other things, but I got you. Oh by the way, I was able to find ya girl."

Trying to listen to Nolan's teacher and him at the same time, she missed the tail end of what he said.

"My bad, I had muted you, Nolan's teacher was telling me about the finger painting they did today. It was too cute, but my apologies. What were you saying again?"

"It's okay. Did you hear me about the reassurance part?"

"I did. You started to say something about oh by the way," she started to say.

"Oh I was saying that I was able to find ole girl."

"Well, I haven't heard from her and she hasn't bothered me, so maybe we should just leave it alone."

"Nova, there's a saying that you would rather be safe than sorry. I want you to know what's going on because it's predominantly your situation. And I also don't want to act without your permission."

"I understand, so what did you find out?" she asked as she headed home.

Omar explained that he managed to do a background check on Ginger. She had a history of females and a few males pressing charges on her for assault, aggravated assault, battery, harassment, and even a few restraining orders. He also discovered that the judge had her on probation, but that sentence was almost up. If she got any more strikes against her the judge would revoke the sentence and have her serve up to twenty years in jail.

He went on to explain that he would only pull the trigger on what she was comfortable with, but refused to just let it further get swept under the rug. Because it was obvious that Ginger was a woman that instead of learning from her mistakes, just found a new victim and Nova was no longer going to be one of them. With the option of filing a restraining order on Ginger or filing a police report, he had someone that would get it in front of the judge so he could see it, and it would potentially send her up the road.

Nova heard her options and did want the luxury of living life with no worries and not feeling paranoid every time she received a new friend request or something odd happened to her. It's not like she could make these filings anonymously, either way she would know, and was just nervous about her seeking revenge. But Omar assured her that either way he had her back.

Knowing he had a special night planned ahead, they agreed to let her think about it and discuss it at a later time. As tonight was special for Nova, she might not have been aware of it, but he did and didn't want to ruin the vibes.

As they arrived at the restaurant with the Atlanta skyline at their view, Nova was speechless yet excited. Between being a mother and working, she didn't get out much and this was a restaurant that was on her list of things to try so it was like he read her mind.

As the host escorted them to their table in the corner of the room that had the best view in Nova's eyes, he pulled out the chair for her. Then lifted Nolan and put him in a booster seat at the table before he took his own seat.

Taking in her surroundings she felt like she was living a dream, but felt her insecurities could quickly damage it all. Especially with what she wanted to ask. Dancing around her own feelings afraid of what he would say or how he would react, she was more in her head than the menu when the waiter came to take their drink orders.

"I want us to try your best red wine," he said as he looked over at Nova. "Unless the beautiful lady across from me would like to start with something else," he added but she didn't hear him.

"Nova," he said to try and get her attention.

"Huh?" she said as she looked up at a loss for words.

"What did you just say? My bad, my mind was elsewhere?" she said .

"Well, whatever happened at work or is bothering you, let's talk about it so I can have your full attention. I don't want to be here and you're here physically but not mentally."

"My bad, I'm okay," she started to say as the waiter came back with two wine glasses and a bottle of wine. "A little wine will help me loosen up some."

"I was going to order Nolan some milk, but I wasn't sure if that was okay or if he could have it or not."

"You're sweet and yes he can. Thank you," she said as she grabbed her wine glass and took a sip.

"I hope I'm not overdoing it," Omar thought to himself as he looked over and admired Nova. "I can't fuck up this time. I almost lost her once because of my immaturity and I refuse to let that happen twice. It's rare nowadays for you to get a second chance. So this is my go big or go home chance," he thought to himself as he sipped his wine before speaking. "So how was your day?" he asked.

"I don't want to be rude, but can we not do small talk? I don't want to juxtapose my past to my present because the two are not matched. I don't want to hold on to what was, but I certainly want to learn from my mistakes and speak up now rather than later. So tell me how you feel, what you're expecting because the stakes are much higher now then when we first met. I want to be receptive to what you're saying and make my decision from there, but what was going on before I can't do. I'm telling you that now. And I can't sit here wanting to enjoy the moment, but in the back of my head I fear I'm only wasting my time yet again," she blurted out.

Taking another sip of his wine as he looked at her and started smiling.

"What?" she asked, confused as to why he was smiling at her.

"I'm smiling because the woman you have become is amazing. I love you're more firm. I hate it took being a part for us both to grow, but it was needed. I'm just thankful that you're giving me another chance. So with that being said," he started to say as the waiter came back to take their orders.

Feeling like she was holding her breath waiting to see what he was about to say had her eager, and the waiter's timing could not have been worse. They all placed their orders and the waiter left, leaving the spotlight back on Omar.

"Like I was saying before he came, umm I ask that you don't judge me on who I was when we first met. I was immature and a little angry at the world. A part of me didn't believe that there was a woman with good intentions. Between how my mom was and the many females that desired me for my looks or what I could do for them, that shit had me with my guard up and heart hard. But when I met you, there was something that just went over me that let me know you were different. For the first time I had found a woman that wasn't like the rest, but I was too in my own way to do you right. So forgive me, but I want to do what I wanted to do before but didn't know how. I want to give you that reassurance and clarity. So with that being said, I wanted to know if we could make it official? Like it sound corny, but fuck it will you be my woman?" he asked as he looked her in her eyes.

Chills went down her spine as she closed her eyes and opened them feeling like she was having an outer body experience.

"I'm sitting here tripping and this man just asked me what I've been wanting to hear for the longest. I was in my feelings scared to ruin the mood and he was already on the same page," Nova thought to herself as she gave a poker face.

"No response?" he asked as she said nothing but just looked at him.

As the waiter came with their food, placed it down, and left, Omar was looking at Nova waiting for her to say something.

"This food looks delicious," she finally said.

"Yes it does, but," he started to say before she cut him off.

"Before you say it let me just get to it... how do you know that you're ready now as opposed to before?" she asked.

"Because in self reflecting, working on me, and honestly not finding fulfillment I knew I had reached my point. I was out here having sex with females and still not feeling a release if that make sense. Like I was catching a nut, but there was nobody I wanted to wake up to, saw a future with, or even considered giving my last name. I was just giving myself away like a free sample. Shit was too toxic and had me questioning myself. Like I felt like I was more and deserved more, but wasn't showing it, so I had to do better."

"I feel that and I hear you," she said and exhaled. Letting out a chuckle, "fuck it, yeah," she continued and started laughing again.

"Why you say it like that?" he asked.

"Because as a hopeless romantic, I can't want love again and be afraid to try again, so I said fuck it, let's do it, and hope that my outcomes be different. Like my grandmother used to tell me when I was younger, you will never know until you try. It just all feels unreal."

"Why though?" he asked.

"Because I never thought you felt like I was good enough for you."

"Shit'd, cap! Cause that's how I felt. I knew you deserved better than me. So when the day came and you told me you were with dude, I couldn't be mad. Though I was, I understood."

"Interesting," she said as she ate and sipped her wine.

"But now you get to be mine fully and my goal is for us to be everything the good Lord desires for us to be."

"Did this man just say the good Lord? I'm about to flood my damn thong," she thought to herself as she squeezed her thighs together.

His words were stimulating her mind and body in ways she never knew he could do, and she was loving it but aimed to try and play it cool.

"Right," she said in response to him and continued to eat and sip her wine.

CHAPTER 15

As the dinner wined down, their plates near cleared, and wine glasses as empty as when they first arrived; they both had smiles from ear to ear staring into each other's eyes.

Omar bit his bottom lip and Nova looked away. She closed her eyes and felt her body swaying and vagina throbbing.

Standing up and walking around to her side of the table, he pulled her chair out and helped her stand. Holding her and looking into her eyes, "now you're off the market and for good this time," he said and kissed her hand.

Taking her free hand waving him off, "stop it. Don't go teasing my head up man," she said.

"Look he's knocked out," he said, shifting his attention to Nolan who had fallen asleep at the table.

"Yeah he is, good thing we're headed home anyhow."

"That's true. Is it okay if I trail y'all home and then I'll head home," he said as he walked around the table to pick up Nolan and put him on his shoulder.

"That's fine," she said as she walked in front of him with him walking behind her to her car.

He put Nolan in his car seat and buckled him in, "go ahead and get in and I'll be right behind you guys."

"Okay," she said as she closed her door and watched him head to his car. Feeling a little sad she drove in silence, no music, and windows up with just her thoughts.

"Instead of overthinking, I should just let things play out. When it comes to life, I'm noticing that that's all we can do. Let it play out. Whatever is meant to happen will. I just want to be happy. I've been through enough ups and downs at this point. I just want a consistent phase of just pure happiness. Then it still bothers me a little that he managed to find that out about Ginger. I guess when I found out about Kaleigh, I didn't really care to dig further. I wonder if I am being considerate of Nolan? I'm not trying to bring just anybody into his life. And I'm not trying to force him to be his Dad. He looks out for him without me even having to ask. Ugh," Nova thought as she made it home. Looking in the rearview mirror to see was Omar still following her and he wasn't behind her.

As she was about to get her phone out to call him, she saw headlights turning in and a vehicle pulled up on the side of her. Unsure if it was him, she locked her doors and stared at the car until the person turned their car off and the door opened.

With Omar's number on stand by, she exhaled as he got out of the car and looked over at her.

Walking around to her side of the door, "you okay? You looked super relieved that this was me. Did you think it was somebody else?" he asked.

"It doesn't matter, you're here now," she said as she looked at him and smiled.

"I promise, that man you needed me to be is going to show up every time. If at any moment I can't, I'm going to figure out how to somehow, do you hear me?"

"Okay," she said as she turned to get out of the car. Before getting out, she pulled him by the shirt and kissed him.

Pulling back and gaining his composure, "damn girl! You should've warned me with that kiss. A second later and I would have had to pull your panties to the side and give it to you in the front seat," he said and started laughing.

"You're funny. I have neighbors and a sleeping kid in the back."

"Neighbors I could care less about, but Nolan you're right. Let's get him in bed."

Walking around to the opposite side of the car to get Nolan, Nova got out of the car and started to head inside with Omar trailing behind her with Nolan on his shoulder. Putting him in his bed and tucking him in before he left out, Nova stood in the door with a smile on her face.

He made a funny face as he noticed Nova standing in the door frame looking at him.

"You were spying on us?" he joked as they fully exited Nolan's room headed for the living room.

"Not really just observing. Never knew you were good with kids."

"I have a little brother and sister that I damn near had to raise on my own, so it comes a little natural."

"That must have been rough for you. I wish I had some siblings. My biological dad has other kids with his wife but we've never met one another."

"Really? That's crazy and rough isn't even the word. I'm glad they had me or shit could've gone real left on a lot of levels, but why are you looking at me like that?"

"Because I'm not used to this emotional and open side of you. I love it but it's definitely different."

"Emotional?"

"Yes, emotional. Opening up and talking about your family. Even though you're not giving the full details, I can tell that was a rough time for you. You know we didn't talk much in the beginning, so this side of you is different for me."

"We did talk girl. Stop that!"

"Yeah about 15%," she said and started laughing. "It was mostly you smashing and dipping with a bullshit excuse attached of how you had to leave all of a sudden every time."

"Damn hearing that from you really makes me sound like I wasn't shit."

"Very often, you weren't," she said and started laughing.

"Why let me continue to do that to you? I'm sorry honestly."

"It wasn't a let, but I wanted you so much that I guess I was letting shit slide when I shouldn't have."

"Just based on the sex?"

"Ha ha ha, sex was a part of it, but I guess I saw the potential in you. The man you could become if you stopped using your dick to stroke your ego. Yes the smash and dip was bad, but I guess I just believed there was more to you."

"Wow, well the sex was pretty damn good, but I wasn't trying to just smash and dip. So many times I wanted to stay and kick it with you. But I wasn't ready to commit to you so I figured by me dipping it would limit either of us catching feelings and it could be just sex. But I never wanted to lose you."

"You damn sure didn't do such a good job," she said and started laughing.

"Again, my apologies," he said as he moved closer to her and took her legs and placed them on him.

"Okay, enough of that for the moment. On the way home, I was thinking about so much and when I didn't see you behind me, I was thinking a little bit of everything. Including what you said about Ginger. I'm tired of assuming the worst when something bad happens in my life. So I want to go forth with doing the restraining order. I deserve to be happy and let that part of my life go."

"Say no more. It'll be done by tomorrow afternoon. I'll keep you updated. Now back to us, can we celebrate?"

"How do you want to celebrate?" she asked as she pulled her legs back from his lap, pulled her dress up and straddled his lap.

Lifting her dress over her head, he squeezed her ass cheeks pulling her more into him as he bit his bottom lip, "I'll take this for sure!"

Beginning to kiss his neck as she could feel his erection in his pants, he unbuttoned her bra freeing her full breast. Leaning back from her succulent lips kissing and sucking on his neck, he unbuttoned his shirt and tossed it to the side.

"Stand up for a min," he said as he stood up slightly to take his pants down and free his throbbing manhood.

For the first time in years since back around each other, they were almost completely naked on the sofa anticipating a moment that had been building. They had sex but this time felt different and better than all the rest. It was like their minds and bodies were in perfect harmony.

The sex was getting so good, she was cumming back to back, squirting, and her eyes were rolled back. She was having one of the best orgasms she had ever had and was enjoying every minute of it. Until he started to slow down.

"What's wrong?" she asked, feeling like her favorite ride at the theme park was closing.

"Nothing, I just want to be able to see that ass in the air, but I want to taste it first. So let's go to the bedroom. Take them panties fully off. I need you on all fours so that pussy can be looking at me," he said and kissed her left breast.

Standing up to head in the bedroom, he smacked her ass, followed behind her, and then closed the door behind them.

Doing exactly as he said and getting into position, he had her with a death grip on the sheets as she grinded her hips and rode his tongue.

"Fuck!" she moaned as she wanted to run but he gripped her thighs to keep her from running.

Wiping his mouth with the back of his hand, he kissed her ass cheeks before inserting himself inside her.

Throwing her ass back in a circle as he stroked in and out her wetness, she began to drool as it felt like he was making love to her g-spot.

"That pussy talking to me like she missed me," he said and smacked her ass. "Throw that shit back how I like it," he added and smacked her ass again.

"I'm cumming," she moaned as her body shook as he continued to stroke in and out of her at an angle.

Smacking her ass again, "turn over."

Turning over on her back, he got on top of her and reinserted himself as he began to kiss her. His strokes were slow, deep, and gentle as if he was making love.

Locking her legs around him as they continued to enjoy each other, she came again. Laying inside her for a minute to catch his breath, he kissed her, pulled out and then laid next to her almost falling asleep instantly.

Trying to find the strength to stand up, she found herself drifting to sleep before she could get up. Feeling like her dream was coming true, she jumped up feeling like it was too good to be true, and he would be gone when she got up. As she panicked and looked to the left of her and as she figured, he was gone. So she thought until she heard the toilet flush, and him coming back in the room with his boxers on and got back in the bed.

"Why are you looking like that?" he asked, noticing the bizarre look on her face.

Exhaling and shaking her head, "nothing," she said and smiled.

"You thought I had left?" he asked as he sat next to her.

Looking at him, "I did unfortunately."

"Ah, that makes sense, but I told you I got you and I'm not that man anymore. I have work tomorrow, but that's later in the morning. I will leave a little before my shift starts so I can get ready, but I will definitely tell you. Hell if I could call out I would because I want to continue to spend all day with you."

Smiling as she looked at him and took in his words, she got up to go pee and felt more confident with his reassurance. When she got back from the bathroom, they cuddled and fell asleep together.

As the morning came they rolled out of each other's embrace but was sleeping soundly until Nova's phone went off startling them both. Trying to find her phone to silence it, she caught a glimpse of the screen and thought it might have been her job calling.

Omar rolled over and pulled her to him just as she was about to answer the phone.

"Let them leave a voicemail," he said as she answered the phone.

Laughing slightly, "Hush, I already answered."

"You're not going anywhere," he said as he held her tighter.

"Stop, Hello," she finally managed to say.

"Well hello to you too," the voice said, causing Nova's eyes to widen and her to sit up quickly, breaking Omar's grip on her.

"Who is this?" she asked, causing Omar to look at her trying to read if she was okay.

"Keiontay, you know Nolan's father," he said.

"Oh hey," she said.

"Sounds like I was interrupting something. Didn't mean to, just was calling to see if I could see my son some time this week. But I think it should be today because I don't appreciate another man being around my son."

"See your son?" she repeated. "And you don't appreciate it," she added.

"Babe, don't get upset," Omar said as he rubbed Nova's back as he figured out who was on the phone based on her responses.

"Keiontay, I have never and will not ever keep you from seeing your son, but I refuse to let you pop in and out when the fuck you feel like it! As far as what you don't appreciate, that man has shown up more for your son than you. You couldn't even call and tell him Happy Birthday! So fuck what you don't appreciate!"

"Nova, I forgot and have had a lot going on. I'll get him something. I'm sorry," Keiontay said, feeling horrible for missing his son's birthday.

"It's cool, he had a great time and didn't notice your absence. That is what matters most!"

"You're right, but can I come by today?"

"Today? That's pretty last minute, I'll have to let you know. Is this a good number to reach you on?"

"Yeah it is and okay, please do, it'll mean a lot to me."

"Un hmm", Nova said and ended the phone call before Keiontay could say anything else.

Laying back down, she just stared at the ceiling.

"I can't make you do anything but if he's trying to truly spend time with him, his actions will show, and you can make your decisions from there. Be the bigger person and leave the door open. Let it never be said that you weren't trying or you stood between them bonding. As a parent, you can do all you can to protect him, but if you reject him coming here it could look like you don't want him to be a part of his life even though that's not the case."

"I just don't want my son to go through the things I did when it came to my dad."

"From having to step in and be the parent to both my siblings, I realized that one of the best ways to raise them is to not operate out of fear. To put my fears on them would be unfair. Life would give them their own, but it was up to me to use what I have been through to better equip them if something of such came up."

"I hear you," she said.

"Plus you don't deserve to do this on your own. I mean you guys have me, but he is his biological father."

"You're right! That's why I love you," she said before realizing what she was saying. "I mean the person you are, love the person you are," she tried to clear up.

"I don't want to jump the gun, but I kind of feel the same and it's crazy. I didn't want to say nothing because I figured I might scare you off or worst you just wouldn't believe me in general."

"What are you saying?"

"I'm saying I love you too Nova Emerson! I have for a while."

Speechless as to what to say next, she was saved with a crying Nolan to tend to.

"Go ahead and tend to him, I'll go make us breakfast before I get ready to head out for work," he said and kissed her on the cheek and then headed to the kitchen.

CHAPTER 16

Keiontay

"She has moved on," Keiontay said to an empty apartment as Morgan had an early shift at the hospital and wasn't back home yet.

"I don't know why I thought she would be waiting on me. Like what about us? What about our family? I know she hadn't heard from me, but to just move on like that and replace me is crazy. But maybe I'm jumping the gun here. Maybe it was a male friend, but she never really hung around anyone for real. Let me not lie to myself, I know what I heard and have to go with my first mind. My son probably won't even know who I am, Keiontay continued to think to himself.

Engulfed in his thoughts, he stared blankly into space at the tv and didn't even flinch as the front door opened.

Morgan walked in from her shift an hour earlier than expected to find Keiontay looking like a deer in the night that just saw a set of headlights.

"Who pissed in your cheerios?" she asked, causing him to come back to reality and notice her presence.

"When did you get in?" he asked.

"Just a few seconds ago, and I'm trying to figure out what's wrong with you. For a minute there I was about to come check your pulse. You had a questionable daze in your eye that made me start thinking the worst."

"Oh nawl, I'm straight, just thinking," he said.

Taking off her shoes and sitting next to Keiontay indian style, facing him, "you sure? Because the tv isn't on and you're holding the air conditioner remote towards the tv. "

"I was about to watch tv," he said.

"Clearly, you didn't get very far," she said and started laughing.

"Obviously," he said and cracked a smile.

"Okay, spit it out, Keiontay because for the short time I've known you, I've never seen you so spaced out like this, what is it?"

"I called my ex today to speak to my son," he started to say.

"Well that's good. How is he or did she not let you talk to him?"

"I mean I asked to see him, not talk to him."

"Well, I'm guessing it was a no and that's the reason you're looking all spaced out and what not."

"She said she would let me know."

"That's not a no, so what's the problem? Get to it man!"

"Before she could say hello when she picked up, I heard a guy's voice in the background."

"Ohhh, baby mama has moved on and it has you in your feelings."

"I guess, but I'm over all shocked and just feel like she just gave up on us. I feel betrayed and like they've replaced me."

"Keiontay, not being funny, but didn't you give up on them the minute you walked out? I don't know every detail of everything, but you're here in an apartment with a stranger basically that you've agreed to move to another state with. So I think it would be fair to say you moved on way before she did. And I can guarantee getting over you was not just a walk in the park for her. As for replacing you, what did you expect to happen? Her to stay miserable and unsure if you'll ever come back? Your son left to not have a father figure. If you heard another guy, the best thing to do is talk about it with her instead of assuming. Then just pray that he's a good guy who's being a good role model for your son."

"Well damn," was all he was able to say.

"That's why you're sitting here looking like you lost your best friend? I can get it but you have to make a decision, either be a man and go home to your family, or continue to do what you're doing and just focus on you."

"So you think I should just focus on myself?"

"I never said that, I said that you need to choose. I can't and won't make that decision for you."

"What about moving to Texas?"

"Keiontay you can't base the decisions I have for my life on what you want to do for you. Even before I met you, I had long ago made that decision. No offense, I won't lose sleep either way because my mind is set on this move as elevation for my life. I won't let nobody deter that for me. You should do the same. Add some structure to your life."

Keiontay said nothing as Morgan's words danced in his head and now added pressure to his decision on what he should do next. He never wanted him and Nova to come to a complete end, but with shutting her out, he can see why she moved on. With her not posting about her new man or giving any indication of talking to anyone, it just came as a shock. He began to wonder if what she and the guy had going on was serious.

"Maybe Morgan is right. Maybe Nova and I should sit down and talk things out. To continue to guess is only a waste of time," he thought to himself.

"I'm going to leave you with your thoughts," Morgan said as Keiontay continued to sit in silence after her last statement as she stood up to leave the room.

"My bad, where are you going?" he asked, noticing her standing.

"To shower, get the feeling of work off of me," she said and left to head to the bathroom.

"Structure in my life huh....if I was able to walk fully what would I be doing? In the streets probably or probably already gone to another state. My goal was to get my money right and dip back out, leaving Nova and Nolan behind. Feeling like they were better off without me anyhow. But here's an opportunity being given to me to do what I was going to do anyway. So maybe this is a sign for me to continue to head in the way I was," Keiontay thought to himself as he looked around the room. "Now not saying anything at all seems easier than I thought. Before I felt a little guilty, but now it doesn't matter," he said as he stood to his feet, grabbed his crutches and headed to the bathroom.

Entering the bathroom to pee, Morgan pulled the shower curtain back to see if she was hearing noises or had Keiontay truly come into the bathroom where she was.

"You okay?" she asked, peeping her head out of the shower to look at him.

"Yeah, just came to pee," he said, standing in front of the toilet preparing to pull his penis out. Forcing Morgan to dart her head back into the shower.

"You could've given me a warning," she said.

"I could've but then you might not have seen this pipe I'm holding."

“Oh you got jokes, because it looked more like a miniature hot dog to me,” she said and they both laughed.

“Oh you funny, but it's good to know you were looking though,” he said as he wiped down the toilet seat and flushed the toilet.

“Oh whatever, hop your way back to the living room,” she said and laughed.

After finishing her shower, she came back into the living room with a Kennasaw State University t-shirt on and some shorts. She sat on the sofa opposite the end from Keiontay.

“So, I was thinking, let me play fix your life,” she stated and they both started laughing.

“Man that was so fucking random, where did that come from Morgan?” he asked.

“I was in the shower thinking that this man needs to get his shit together. It’s not like it’s impossible. He just needs some direction, and I’m no expert nor is my life perfect, but I can help where I can.”

“Oh really, it's not like I really have any other choice really,” he said with a smirk. “So what’s first Ms. Morgan fix my life?”

“Well, did you ever have a career or were you always doing what you were that put you in this current situation?”

“Well, I was into soccer and engineering, but life happened and things took a detour. Simple as that,” he said and humped his shoulders.

“So since you’ve fallen out of those careers, you’ve had no desire to go back to either of those things? Either one sounds promising depending on how good you were at soccer.”

“I mean Nova tried to encourage me to go back into my profession, but I didn’t believe in myself enough and wanted the quick route. I should’ve listened, but hey.”

“That is the first time I've heard you say her name. She sounds like she has your best interest at heart, but it’s not like it’s the end for you Keiontay. You talk like you’re giving up on life entirely when you’re young and have so much to offer. It just sounds like the girl you thought had your child caused you to doubt your own abilities. Her toxicity overshadows your potential to grow, which is unfair. If she’s no longer a part of your life, step out of those shadows and rebuild you and be better.”

“Girl you might be on to something,” he said and smiled. “You might be in the wrong profession, got damn but I hear you. I have to find myself again for sure. I definitely have lost sight of myself dealing with her and her bullshit.”

“It’s often said to women but not to men enough, regain your power!”

“I appreciate you for that and I needed to hear that! So what’s next?”

“Create five focus points for your life and make them your priority. No certain order, just things to hold yourself accountable. Include nothing that anybody else wants for you or how they should see you. Nothing but what you want for you. I can’t decide for you. I can only give you that advice and hope that you take it in and do what resonates within.”

“I feel that,” he started to say as he received a notification on his phone from Nova that caught his attention. Talking to Morgan had really gotten his mind off of the situation, but Nova’s text just brought the moment back into focus.

“Everything okay?” Morgan asked, noticing Keiontay distracted from their conversation.

“Ah yeah, just got a text from Nova,” he said and continued to look at his phone unsure of what to do.

“So are you going to read it?” she inquired. “Instead of guessing what it says, just open it,” she added.

Keiontay said nothing and opened the message fighting through his what if’s.

Nova: Hey, I gave it some thought and I don’t want to stand in the way of you spending time with Nolan. He deserves to spend time with you and vice versa. I think it would be good for the both of you honestly. We don't have much planned for today, so if you're free, we can meet up somewhere around 5pm. What do you think?

Keiontay read the message about three times and still fell short of the right words to respond with. A part of him wanted to jump at the opportunity. While the other half considered maybe living well enough alone. But then fighting against his fears of doubt, he took into consideration Morgan's words and decided that being a better father would be one of his focus points. The meet up would be his first step in the right direction.

Keiontay: Hey, thank you for reaching back out and I would love that. 5pm works fine, but where do you want to meet?

Nova: You want to go to the neighborhood park that's by my place? They have a good playground that I'm sure he would love. It would be a lot for you guys to do.

Keiontay: Sounds good. I'm looking forward to it, thank you. See you guys soon.

Looking up from his phone Keiontay smiled, feeling accomplished towards the first step of turning his life around.

"Conversation must have gone pretty good the way you're smiling," Morgan said, noticing his smile.

"I think so. So, what do you have planned for today," he asked her.

"Umm I was thinking we could try that new restaurant they just opened up last week, what do you think?" she asked.

"Um, I kind of just made plans so will tomorrow be okay?"

"Sure, I'll just grab something else then and probably watch a movie. I probably just need to chill for today anyhow. So she's letting you see him today?"

"Yes, but I need a ride. As you can tell I'm not in the best predicament to be driving currently."

"So, you want me to drop you off to be with your baby mother and son. You think that's a good idea?"

"Nova isn't like that, plus it's not like I'm rolling up with my girlfriend or somebody I'm smashing. The first time I did that was disrespectful enough."

"Right," Morgan said dryly as his words stung a little.

Catching on to her tone of voice, "I don't mean that you couldn't be just saying," he tried to clear up.

"It's cool, I get what you meant. So what time are you guys supposed to meet? Also, does she know about your current situation?" she inquired.

"5pm and that I'm staying with you? No, nobody really knows where I am honestly and I want to kind of keep it that way," he stated.

"If that doesn't raise my eyebrows, I don't know what does. You said that like there's something you left out that I could be blind sided by. Because I wasn't actually talking about the living arrangements, but you recovering and being on crutches."

"Ah damn you right," he said, realizing that he wouldn't be able to run behind his son at the park. Being indoors would be better since he would be able to sit in one spot or do minimal movement.

"So I take it that she doesn't know that either or probably what even happened to you?" she asked.

"Ah naw."

"Wow, so I guess you're going to have to come clean now with everything. Which is not too bad of a thing. It could probably help the both of you."

As Morgan's words entered his ears, he had an epiphany. He wasn't ready to explain to Nova his decisions and what he had planned next.

"If she sees me like this, she's going to be more disappointed in me or probably feel guilty. I don't want to make her feel like that. And I don't want Nolan to see me like this. What was I thinking? Damn, I just feel like I keep fucking up," Keiontay thought to him self as Morgan had turned silent.

Keiontay looked at his phone and debated if he should reach out to Nova and let her know of his change of heart. However, he figured that too would draw a magnitude of questions he again was not ready to answer. And sure as hell was not in the mood to argue. So he turned his phone off and put it in his pocket.

Breaking the silence of the room, "so you still want to go to that restaurant?" he asked, grabbing Morgan's attention.

"Yeah, you said we can go tomorrow and I said that was cool. Did you forget already?" she asked as she looked at him.

"Right, but we can go ahead and go today. It's not like either of us is doing anything plus it beats sitting in the house all day," he stated.

"Man, are you losing it! You just asked me to drop you off so you can see your son today! What is going on with you? You might need a MRI for your brain the way you are acting," she said and started laughing.

"Ha ha ha, very funny. Naw I just don't want to leave you hanging, we can go to the restaurant."

"Did she cancel on you? Cause if so that's messed up. Hopefully she at least gave you a good reason why because you were excited I can tell," she inquired.

Debating if he should be honest and correct her because that wasn't the case. It was more so him standing in the way of his own self. Thinking he was going to get judged for his current situation. He rather not face them and decided to lie. In his mind, the less he had to explain the better.

"Yeah, she did and no she didn't say why. She just said that something came up, and we would have to meet up another time."

"That's so messed up, I'm sorry she got your hopes up like that. Sounds like she might still be bitter and is trying to hurt you," she stated and then went into her bedroom to start getting dressed.

"I guess so," Keiontay said under his breath. He picked up his phone and debated on if he should at least let Nova he wasn't coming. That seemed like the right thing to do since he couldn't pull himself together to tell her what was really going on. Although he hated lying to her and letting it seem like Nova was this bitter baby mama how most are depicted, it was easier to let her look like the bad guy than him seeming incapable to do the bare minimum.

"I shouldn't have reached out in the first place. I don't know what I was thinking," he thought to himself. Deciding to avoid the situation all together, he went in his contacts and placed her on block.

CHAPTER 17

"Don't you have to take that car back soon or did you get the rental time extended?" Tarven asked Ginger as she was in the kitchen making her some coffee before heading to work.

"Huh?" Ginger asked as she was in a daze. She looked in the cabinets for her favorite mug as she waited for him to repeat what he had initially said.

"It's in the dishwasher. I haven't gotten a chance to unload it yet this morning. But I said don't you have to take the rental car back soon?"

"Oh, yeah, that's right but maybe I'll get it extended for a little while longer," she said thinking that she had yet to get the license plate number so she could find out more information.

"Babe, that's a waste of money when you have a car of your own and the windows are fixed now . So just return it, unless it's a part of my surprise that you're working on," he said as he walked up behind her and grabbed her waist from behind.

"Surprise?" she asked, feeling confused.

“Don’t act like you don’t know what I’m talking about. I want to be surprised so you don’t have to tell me,” he said as he kissed her on her neck. Then walked back into the bedroom to get ready for work.

As she mixed her coffee in her favorite mint green ceramic mug, she stirred and thought that she would book him a spa day or some. Use some of her savings and buy him something nice for once and a while, and that would take care of the supposed surprise she was said to have. However, her main focus was to get the license plate number, go on about her day, and stop having to sneak around.

As she finished her coffee she grabbed her purse, kissed Tarven and said she was headed to work. Though she told the truth, she just wasn’t headed to work at the precise moment he thought. She called into the office and told the staff she would be there, but had a family emergency with her daughter to handle first.

They understood and off Ginger headed to the apartments. She was steps closer to figuring out what was going on with Keiontay, with the small possibility of getting things back on track. In her mind they could work things out. Then to fix everything, she would give him a child. She even had intentions to propose. If that was what it took to show him how serious she was about him and their possibility of a future.

"You ready?" Morgan asked as came out of her bedroom dressed in some fitted stone wash jeans, printed front tie shirt, and some white Alexander McQueen sneakers.

"Ready for what?" Keiontay asked as he took his attention from the tv screen and looked at Morgan. "Don't you look nice," he said before she could speak.

"Your follow-up doctor's appointment," she stated as she looked at the time.

"Damn you right, I thought it was next week, I'm tripping. Um, I can just go with what I have on then shower and change when we get back."

"If you say so, I think you have enough time to at least change your draws, put on another shirt, and brush your teeth," she suggested.

Laughing slightly at her suggestions, "I'll take the hint and change my ass out of these clothes."

"I'm just saying, it doesn't hurt to not look like what you're going through," she said as she went into the kitchen to make her a smoothie.

"You could've been the only one of us that looked good, and that would have been fine with me," he stated as he searched through his duffle bag for an outfit.

“Ha ha no,” she said as she started to place frozen strawberries, mangoes, and bananas into the blender.

“Shawty said I wasn’t about to make her look bad,” he joked as he started taking off the white t-shirt he had on.

“I mean that’s partially true, but how you present yourself to the world even in your everyday attire can say alot. You and I both know that as a Black person and as a Black man especially, we don’t need to give them any extra excuses to jump when they feel froggy.”

“You right,” he said as he put on a black Nike graphic t-shirt, some black Nike joggers, black socks, and matching slides. “I had forgotten all about my appointment to be honest,” he added as he sat back down after getting ready.

“I can tell, but I kind of figured which is why I got off a little early,” she said as she grabbed her car keys, purse, and headed for the door.

“Hold on, I need to find my wallet,” he said as he patted his pockets realizing he didn’t have it on him.

While Morgan helped Keiontay search for his wallet, on the other side of town, Tarven was out picking up and dropping off customers. The daycare called to inform him that he needed to come and pick up Kaleigh from daycare. She had thrown up, and messed up her clothes.

They also shared that they tried to call her mother first, but her office had said she wasn't in at the moment which is why they called him.

Tarven knowing that his daughter's well being is important, he dropped off the customer at their destination and floored it to the daycare to take care of his daughter. A great part of him was pissed and the other half confused as to what the hell was going on with Ginger. As he drove to the daycare, he tried calling Ginger but the phone just rang as if she wasn't near her phone. So he decided to call her job and maybe the daycare workers were wrong, and it was all a misunderstanding.

"Hey, may I speak to Ginger?" Tarven asked as the receptionist answered the phone.

"May I ask who's calling?" she responded.

"Tarven, her child's father," he stated.

"Ah, Mr. Wesley, hey! I knew that sounded like you, but she's not in at the moment. She called in a while ago to let us know she would be a few hours late coming in as she had a situation to deal with you guys daughter. I hope everything is okay."

"Wait, what? How she? So she said she had an, you know what okay, gotcha," Tarven said as he was piecing the pieces together from what the receptionist said.

"Did I say something wrong?" the receptionist asked.

"No, not at all, I had just thought she had made it back to the office by now since I had stepped in," Tarven said. "I had just wanted to ask her something, but I'll wait a little later and try again."

"You sure? I can take down a message for her to call you."

"Yes, do that please," he stated.

"Will do," she said and he hung up before she could say anything else.

As he arrived at the daycare, he tried calling Ginger again, but the phone just rang. Hanging up the phone, he shook his head and could only imagine what she was out doing.

"I don't want to hear shit about she out doing some fucking surprise because you den lied on our fucking child. And now she's actually fucking sick, and her ass can't be reached," he thought to himself as he headed in the facility to get Kaleigh to take her home.

Morgan found Keiontay's wallet on the floor slightly under the sofa, and just in time so they wouldn't be late for his appointment. But what they didn't know is that they still had a rude awakening ahead. As they headed for the front door to leave, they opened the door and were shocked to see the same black car parked behind her car as before. The only difference this time is that Morgan saw the person taking a picture of the back of her car. As Keiontay stepped out further to see why Morgan had stopped in her tracks, he yelled, “man what the fuck?” causing Morgan to look at him in shock and the car to drive off once they seen and heard him.

“I take it that had something to do with you?” Morgan asked. “Who was that and do I need to be worried?”

Rubbing his hand over his face and shaking his head, “ honestly, I wouldn’t say worried, but she certainly can’t be fucking trusted.”

“Was that your baby mother?” she inquired.

“Hell naw.”

“Then who was it then Keiontay? I hardly associate with anyone outside of my friends, and that was neither one of them. So there’s no reason why a female I don’t know should be darkening my fucking door step!”

“You remember that toxic ex I was telling you about? Her.”

“You didn’t give me the full story so I think now is a good time to elaborate. Because being toxic and dangerous are two different things. And honestly, I don’t have time for either. I’m sorry but if she is a part of your life and is going to bring drama in my life, I won’t be able to continue to let you stay here.”

Hitting his fist into his hand, filled with frustration, “Damn man, I’m so fucking tired of this girl. I haven’t talked to her since everything went down about her lying about her daughter being mine. I was hoping when I ran into Tarven that he wouldn't say anything to her, but I see he did. I'm going to fix it, I promise. She won't bother you. I promise I'm going to handle it, please trust me, give me a chance to make things right," he pleaded.

"I'm not sure who Tarven is or whoever, but if she comes back around her again I'm throwing in the towel. And you're going to have to go."

"I understand," he said.

"Now, let's go before we're later than what they accept and won't see you," she said as she headed to the car with Keiontay on her trail.

Unsure of what to say on the drive to his appointment, he remained quiet leaving Morgan the chance to vocalize her thoughts.

"Me taking in a stranger isn't the brightest thing to do, but I felt I was helping you. I wasn't lonely or desperate for some male attention. If I wanted some guy to lay under me, I'm sure there's a dime a dozen that I would have no problem getting in contact with," she stated firmly.

Keiontay remained silent because he figured she wasn't done.

"Like how the hell did she even find me? You? She's probably been stalking you this whole time. I've heard of bitches being dickmatized, but that's too much what is the point even. Do you not hear me talking or do you now not have anything to say about this bullshit?"

Before Keiontay could answer, she continued vocalizing her thoughts, "Like I've had some good dick in my life but I'm no stalker. A glance at a guy's social media maybe, but even now that's played out. Especially if a man isn't checking for me, I'm giving you the same energy you give me. Because if a man shows me he doesn't want me, I'm not about to force him to want me. Dick isn't everything especially when I have much more to offer."

"As you should," Keiontay finally said, causing Morgan to look at him out of the corner of her eye. "What?" he asked, noticing her side glare.

"Cause I don't get it, why is she stalking you so much?"

"Damn you make it seem like I ain't shit at all or have nothing going for myself," he said feeling defensive.

"I mean you're living with a stranger and was living in a hotel room, so from the outside looking in it doesn't seem like much to be chasing after no offense. Maybe when y'all two were together and maybe you have the potential to be great, but right now I haven't seen much. You're attractive I'll give you that and maybe even slang some good D. Hell, I guess it's to each's own because even if you were a millionaire I still wouldn't be running behind you or stalking you. That's just me."

“Well damn, I would say thanks for the compliment but it seems a little redundant at this point.”

“I mean, the shit just pisses me off and I’m not trying to take it out on you, but this problem stems from you. I want you to get your shit together! Not for anybody else but for your damn self. From what you told me and what happened before we left screams the repercussions for a lack of accountability.”

Keiontay said nothing and began to scroll through his phone to see if he still had Tarven's number and realized he didn’t. As he started to tune out Morgan because he felt like she was attacking him verbally and putting him down, he focused on figuring out how Ginger found him. Beginning to scroll on social media to find Tarven’s account, he messaged him and asked him to call him immediately through the app as it was important.

In the midst of the awkwardness since Keiontay responded with silence to her statement, Keiontay's phone rang and it was Tarven.

“What’s going on man? You straight, I didn’t think I would be hearing from you anytime soon,” Tarven said as Keiontay answered.

“Man, honestly you probably weren't until what just went down led to me having to reach out to you,” he stated.

“What do you mean? You straight? I can come by the hotel if you need me to, I’ll be on that side in like an hour.”

"Hmm, so you think I'm still at the hotel?"

"I mean that's the last place I took you. I just assumed that's where you still were," he stated.

"Beat, but that lets me know that you're probably in the dark about what's going on. Ginger just pulled up on me and now shawty pissed and I don't blame her. There is no reason why she should still be following or stalking me and shit! Like maybe I assumed wrong. I thought since she's your kid and I wasn't in the picture that y'all was together, and I wouldn't have to worry about her crazy ass ways anymore. Because frankly I can't handle that shit right now!" he said with hostility.

Before Tarven could say anything, Keiontay heard him put the phone down and yell, "fuck!" in the background. Seconds later, he returned to the phone and tried his best to talk calmly but he was filled with rage and wanted to strike . Despite the love he has for Ginger, he knew that Keiontay wasn't lying and it all made sense. He just wanted to know when it all started. Because he felt stupid for thinking he had nothing to worry about, and trusting to tell her about his run in with Keiontay. He started feeling regretful in saying anything, but her assurance led him to believe she was over him; however, it was all a front.

"How could I be so stupid!" he yelled and grunted.

"Yo!" Keiontay said, trying to get Tarven's attention.

Trying to regain his composure, "my bad man, just had a harsh slap in the face of reality just then. I can't lie man, but she played me too. She told me she was over you and that it was us when I did tell her I saw you. I thought she was over the game of trying to have her way on both ends. But I see she's back on the war path to try and reclaim what she thinks she deserves. I can't do this shit any more. Treating me like I'm not good enough for her that she has to have you too. So how she found you bro, I don't know. My only guess is she's either been snooping through my shit or following you or hell even me or all thee above. You can sometimes never know with her," he explained.

"Man, I hear you, but you said you still got my back and I need you to have it now. Reel her in, talk to her or some cause if not I might have to go another route at this point. She's affecting too many people in my life and that shit isn't fair to me nor them!"

"I hear ya bruh, I'm going to handle it for sure. You don't have anything to worry about. I see this bitch stripes haven't changed, she just played her role," he stated. "Wait, when did this happen?"

"Not too long ago! We was headed out and this car was parked behind shawty car. She had seen the same car a few days ago, but we thought nothing of it and I never would've thought it was her. It wasn't her car so I didn't think it could be her, then when I peeped it was her she drove off. Like come on, I den saw yo dumb ass now," Keiontay was saying until he paused talking mid sentence.

"Hello," Tarven said, trying to see if the call had dropped.

"Yeah, I'm still here, just thinking!" Keiontay said. "I wish I had been dead this shit!"

"Right! Cause she too fucking grown to keep doing the same thing! I can do better and my daughter definitely deserves a better mother. I think it's time we handle our shit bruh."

"I couldn't agree more," Keiontay said as he paused and reflected on his life. He too needed to get things together sooner than later. As the phone grew silent, Keiontay said, "aye man, before you go, if you love that little girl like I did or I hope even more knowing that she is yours, save her, and stop letting her see all of Ginger's toxicity. She might be little and not able to voice what she's seeing and how it makes her feel, but it could damage her in the long run. One of the reasons I stayed way longer than I should have when it came to all of Ginger's bullshit is to protect Kaleigh. I wanted to be her shield as much as possible. I can't encourage you to raise her like I was doing, but I am kind of asking you to consider her when it comes to fixing all this drama. Because I can only be accountable for my actions and you the same. It's about time she starts to see the consequences of her actions."

"I couldn't agree more bruh. You honestly just put something into consideration that I never truly ever thought about. It even completely changes what I was thinking to do. So I appreciate that for real. Be careful out here man, " Tarven said as the phone grew back silent.

"You too, I gotta go," Keiontay said and the call ended. They had arrived at his doctor's appointment. Ready to face the updates about his progress he was eager to get out of the car. Morgan tagged behind feeling a new found respect for Keiontay.

She now understood what it was that could possibly have this crazed woman stalking this man, his heart. It was big and beautiful, he just was not the best at making decisions. And that reminded her of herself more than she realized. She decided at that moment to receive the blessing she had been sent, then so quickly to give it away as she was ready to do before hearing his phone call.

CHAPTER 18

Keiontay's words danced in Tarven's head, but the anger and betrayal was still so fresh that it was hard to shake. He was at the crossroads of being mature about the situation and being fed up. Irrationally thinking, he took the lower route with the first step being him making a call to Ginger.

Driving away from a chaotic moment with the technicality of getting caught, she was still smiling from ear to ear as she had finally gotten what she wanted. To see Keiontay and get the license plate number of the girl he seemed to be living with. With a smile planted on her face, she headed to work to go about her regular routine as though she hadn't just stalked a stranger and him for damn near a week. As she walked in the doors of the office to clock in and start her day, the staff immediately asked if everything was okay.

Filled with excitement, she said, "yes," not thinking about what they were asking about and walked away. In no mood to mix her personal life with her work life, she just started seeing patients as scheduled.

After knocking out a patient and about to start on the second, her dental assistant stepped out of the room. She then came back in with a message from the receptionist that her child's father was on the phone. In no mood to deal with Tarven, she told them to tell him that she would call him back later. Before relaying the message the dental assistant mentioned to Ginger that it could be about your daughter again.

Completely overstepping her work-life boundaries with Ginger, Ginger stopped in her tracks and gave the assistant a look that let her knew she had fucked up. Taking her evil glare as a firm answer, the assistant went to relay the message. But came back with a message for Ginger from Tarven that said, "either you come to the phone now or I come to you. The choice is yours how you decide for this to go."

"Did he sound angry?" Ginger asked the assistant as Tarven's message raised an alert in her that he was pissed about something. "Maybe it's irritation from thinking about the surprise I said I was putting together for him. Some people get overly anxious, especially him, so I'll just deal with him when I get home. Plus I can't wait to take a break to find out more information on ole girl. Connect some dots in this situation," Ginger thought to herself

"I mean I couldn't really tell, he seemed calm. Plus I didn't want to pry too much into it after the mistake I just made," the assistant explained.

"Okay, you're excused, I'll deal with it later. What time is my next patient?" Ginger asked before the assistant stepped out of her presence.

"In about forty five minutes. Do you need me to reschedule that patient?"

"No, it's fine. Just wanted to check on something. I'll be in my office until the patient arrives," Ginger said and they went their separate ways. Elated with the way things were unfolding, she had enough time to go into her office and see what she could find. Going into her office and closing the door, she immediately opened her laptop. Opened the first search engine she could, and searched the public database she used when she wanted to be nosey for certain information.

As she typed in her license plate number and the state, paid the database release fee, she unlocked the information she wanted. She found out her name and address, and from there she went to her social media profiles to cross reference further information. She uncovered where Morgan went to school, where she worked, and places she visited. In under thirty minutes she had hit the jackpot for the information she had been hunting for.

"She's a nurse huh?" Ginger said as she looked at the screen of a picture of Morgan in her scrubs at work. As she studied the screen, she thought about reaching out to her friend at the hospital to pull Keiontay's chart to see if she was his nurse.

Engulfed in her mission to get her questions answered, she called her friend and it confirmed what she was thinking. Morgan was one of the nurse's that he had while he was admitted. Now why he was with her was another mystery; however, for now she was content with the information she had. Her next plan was to find a way to contact Keiontay so she could apologize again. Then everything could go back to how things used to be.

With only a few minutes left on her break before the next patient, she continued to scroll through Morgan's social media pictures until she heard a knock at the door.

Before she could finally get up to see who was at the door, it flew open with Tarven standing in the frame of the door.

Shocked at his presence, "Babe!" she said as she looked at him and smiled.

Tarven said nothing as he walked in and closed the door behind him.

"Where's Kaleigh?" she asked, trying to get him to say something, but he remained silent as he looked around the room.

"So, you're a psychic now?" he said, finally speaking.

"What are you talking about?" she asked.

"You knew Kaleigh was going to be sick or did you just lie on an innocent baby for your own sick and selfish ass reasonings?" he asked as walked close to Ginger barely giving her any room to move.

"I," Ginger started to say, but Tarven's hand was around her throat before she could say anything else.

"You are a sick and ungrateful ass bitch! I swear on my entire soul, I want to knock your fucking head through one of these walls, but you're not worth the jail time. I told you whatever you were doing in the dark was going to come out! You fucking played me, I'm still not enough for you," Tarven said as he tightened his grip around her throat causing her to try and pull his hand away.

Thinking he was going to choke the life out of her in her office, tears rolled down her face as she began to lose consciousness. Releasing his grip, Ginger fell to the floor gasping for air.

"Don't even utter the words that you're sorry because it already shows. You lied to me, and you lied on our daughter for fucking Keiontay. You looked me in my face and lied! You pretended you were over him! Since I told you about running into him, you probably have been tracking his every move. You had me believing that finally the woman I loved, loved me back. I promise I want to stomp you as you're down because you disgust me. Luckily the same man that you'll risk it all for gave me some great words of advice. He calmed a part of me that was filled with rage much worse than this, and he was right. I hope it was worth it because with everything in me, you will no longer be a part of our lives and that's on Kaleigh," he said as a tear rolled down his face. He went in his pocket and threw a box at Ginger before he turned and walked out the door leaving her behind on the floor.

As she watched him leave, she rolled to her side and laid on the floor in the fetal position. Enjoying the chance to breathe freely, she reached for the box, and opened it to find a ring inside. With a single tear cascading down her face, she started laughing as she found more humor in the situation than tragedy. And in the same swift motion took the box and threw it as her only thoughts were that she hated she got caught.

"Marriage? Please, unless I could marry them both, I would never. His feelings still would have been hurt cause I most likely would have said no. He's not a bad guy, it's just to me, he's better for me when Keiontay is in the picture that's all," Ginger thought to herself as she sat up on the floor looking around the room.

With her break at its end, her assistant came to knock on her door, but was shocked to find Ginger on the floor. "Are you okay?" she asked in panic. "Did he do something to you? Do I need to call the police?" she added as she began to help Ginger up off of the floor.

Ignoring her assistant's questions, "is the patient here yet?" Ginger asked as she brushed past her assistant to the examination room.

In that room was Ginger's personal life that had just exploded in her face, so she was more than happy to get back to work and put it all on the back burner. However, though she was in another room, her thoughts were still with her. She wondered how Tarven had put it all together. Was Tarven thinking about taking Kaleigh from her, and most importantly was Keiontay mad at her.

While Ginger worked to finish her shift, she hoped that as the day came to a close everything would have worked itself out. As she saw no wrong in her actions. To her, she was just a woman in love and wanted Keiontay to understand that she was willing to do anything to be with him. With Tarven, she loved him but trying to get to that level of being in love with him was hard. But it was also hard to just let him go. In her mind, her happiness was when they both were a part of her. But knowing Keiontay was back in town and where he was now, she felt it wouldn't be long before everything she wanted and how she wanted would be back in place. What she didn't factor in is that the wave she was riding was about to crash.

Tarven had gone back to their place and packed up some of his stuff and Kaleigh's. Picked her up from his cousin and then headed back to his apartment that he had never gotten rid of. He kept his apartment as a safe haven and right now the timing could not be more perfect. He had packed up most of what his daughter had so she could have it there and all she didn't, he would get. His mind was scattered and emotions were on edge as his love life was now back in pieces. All while he was about to commit to being a full time single father.

He told Ginger nothing and figured it would be the perfect payback if she cared any. Or it could be a complete bust and she sees it as more of a relief than a problem. She didn't tell him about her sneaking around, so he wouldn't tell her about their whereabouts.

He figured if she figured it out and came to his apartment he wouldn't answer the door and overall just hoped she wouldn't come when they were at home. Plus, within the week he was going to put in for a two bedroom apartment on the property or at one of their associating apartments. Then going to switch his daughter's daycare, block Ginger's number, and go to the court to file for full custody. He had reached his breaking point with Ginger finally and was tired of being her second choice and their daughter an afterthought.

Taking on so much responsibility and changes at once was overwhelming, but well overdue. At some point, he realized that once everything unfolded Ginger would surely be beyond pissed. He cared less now about her feelings and felt it was something she well deserved.

On another spectrum, Omar's promise of having Nova's back was something he was serious about fulfilling. Once she had agreed to pull the trigger and let Ginger's karma unravel how it may, he put in a couple of special favors and got the restraining order expedited. With Ginger's history and a judge that was no fan of domestic violence and harassment, Ginger's serving day was in motion. In the midst of a good laugh with a patient, the receptionist came to the back and asked if she could come to the front for a minute as a situation needed her attention. Unsure of what was so urgent that she had to be pulled away from a patient, she froze as she opened the door to the waiting room where a sheriff stood with an envelope in his hand.

Ginger's first thought was panic as the sheriff asked her first and last name to confirm she was who he was looking for. As she anticipated the words that were about to leave his mouth, her heart raced.

"Is my daughter okay?" she asked before he could get out the reason for his visit. She immediately started to feel guilty that something could have happened to her daughter or Tarven and they had just gotten into an argument. Tears started to form in her eyes thinking the worst.

"Ma'am, I'm not here on behalf of any loved ones, you've been served," he said sternly as he extended the envelope to her.

Frozen in her tracks and dried traces of tears on her face, Ginger was shocked, relieved yet embarrassed. With the office staff and patients focused on what was transpiring, Ginger took the envelope and went straight to her office and slammed the door. Reaching her chair to sit down before opening the envelope, her heart raced as she ripped it open and pulled out papers that notified her a restraining order had been filed against her. The order stated that she had to stay three hundred feet from Nova Emerson, the victim's home, job, car, and school and those associating with her for three hundred and sixty five days with the start date being the day of being served unless further extended.

"What a little bitch!" Ginger screamed. "She just gave me another fucking strike on my name!" she said to an empty room as anger filled her. "I want to beat her ass! Fucking bitch! I still need to get her ass back for shooting my ass that day like she was really about that life. I was not harassing her scary ass! So damn scary, but she ain't the first one, it's cool. I've gotten around this type of shit before and I'll do the same again if I need to. Lucky for her, I'm more irritated by the office and patients being in my business, but I have bigger shit at hand at the moment. I'll deal with this later," she continued to say as she grabbed her belongings and headed for the front door to go home for the day.

In the parking lot, she tried to call Tarven to see where he was so they could talk about the ring. Then find out what all he knew, and tell him about Nova's restraining order, but he didn't answer. Instead her call went directly to voicemail. Figuring maybe he was in the middle of calling somebody else, she tried calling back and the same thing happened. After the third, fourth, and fifth attempts, she tried texting him, but her texts did not deliver. Thinking that he possibly blocked him, she tried calling *69 but the phone just rang. Starting to get frustrated she decided to just head home and confront him there about blocking her.

The only problem was when she finally got home, Tarven nor Kaleigh were there as she expected. She threw her belongings down and searched the house, but found nothing but things missing and some drawers empty. Getting back angry, she screamed and tried calling Tarven again only to get his voicemail.

"Where the hell are you?" she yelled in the first voicemail to Tarven.

Calling back, "Tarven un-fucking-block me!" she yelled in a second voicemail.

"Can you at least tell me if Kaleigh is with you?" she said in a third voicemail.

"Tarven, I'm sorry!" she said in her fourth voicemail.

"I need to know you both are okay. I know I messed up. Is she okay? Where are you guys, I'll come to you. We can get through this," she said in a fifth voicemail.

"Naw, fuck that, you want to play these fucking games! I can play them better! I'm glad this shit is over. I just want my fucking child. You don't deserve to be in her life," she said in a sixth voicemail.

"I'm sorry, I didn't mean that, I'm just angry. I love you both," she said in a seventh voicemail before deciding to visit the places that Tarven normally does in hopes of running into them.

"If I have to drive all night, I'm going to find you," Ginger said as she changed her clothes, grabbed her purse, keys, and headed out the front door. The first stop on her hunt was Tarven's old apartment.

CHAPTER 19

Nova began to prepare her plans for the day around meeting Keiontay; she was nervous that they might argue, but prayed that it all turned out different. She didn't want to argue with him, she just wanted Nolan to spend time with his Dad. With the hope of getting better at communicating for the sake of co-parenting. Then they could go on about their day. She was willing to try, which is why she listened to Omar and had even agreed to them spending time together.

She thought about reaching out to him to confirm him still showing up, but figured when the time got closer she would do so. However, there was a great part of her that believed he wouldn't show, but she brushed it off in believing that she didn't want her own personal experiences of disappointment from her biological father to spill into her son's life. So she ignored her doubt and got them both ready. A part of her had got a little excited to see if Nolan would even recognize him, if he would just see him as a stranger, or would be friendly either way. Her hopes were that it all just worked out for the best.

As time neared, she left out thirty minutes prior to meeting so she could avoid traffic. On the way there, she called Omar who told her that if she needed him, he was only a call away. As well as, he was proud of her for being mature about the situation, and hoped that Nolan would have a good time. He also informed her that Ginger had been served today and asked how she felt.

Completely thrown off with the Ginger statement, she brushed it off and said that it was good and thanked him for his support. As she ended the call, she found the number Keiontay had called from. She called it to see how far away he was, but she didn't get an answer.

Keiontay had completed his follow up visit and was grateful about the news that he was healing up just fine. And was looking at a possible shorter recovery time with the way his body was healing.

With the weight of regret and embarrassment on his mind, despite his good news he just nodded his head. Morgan was confused as she listened to the doctor's notes and comments. She thought he would be much happier at what he had told him.

When the doctor left out and told him he would see him back in two weeks for some follow up x-rays, Morgan took that moment to address Keiontay's impassiveness.

"I know what happened before we left the house was a bit much, but this moment is about you. Why are you not showing more emotion about what he said?" she asked.

"I just have a lot on my mind right now honestly," he replied. " We can head out right?" he added.

Grabbing him by the arm, "Keiontay, you're no genie! I don't expect you to blink your eyes and snap your fingers and everything to be fixed. I know things take time. I just was saying that I don't want drama in my life. I don't deserve that especially when it doesn't in any way include me."

"You right," he said dryly.

"Now you are boxing me out," she stated with an attitude.

"Naw, I just think you're right and I've overstayed my welcome. I do have too much going on. So when we get back to your house, do you mind taking me to a nearby hotel?"

"I never said you had to leave," she stated.

"It's cool, I just need to handle all of this on my own."

"No offense, you've been doing it on your own and shit hasn't been panning out too well for you."

"Then what am I supposed to do, Morgan? You seem to have a lot of the answers for my life."

"Look, don't get smart with me. I don't have the answers for your life. I'm just saying to take your guard down. Start letting somebody help dig you out of what you got going on. Hell, even Superman had a sidekick."

Laughing at her corniness, he pulled her to him and gave her a hug. As she hugged him back, his cologne mind chills run down her spine. A part of her was ready to throw her caution to the wind and see what all the fuss was about, and the other half of her wanted to just keep it platonic. Stepping out his embrace, she stepped to the side, and they headed out of the doctor's office.

As she walked beside him, "you want to go get some ice cream for having a good doctor's report?" she asked him as they took their time back to her car.

"I'm not a kid, plus we're going to eat in a little bit right?"

"Yes, but like you said, you're not a kid and ice cream isn't going to spoil your appetite I'm sure."

"Man you are different for sure."

"Maybe, so are you a chocolate kind of guy or vanilla?"

While Keiontay and Morgan headed to eat ice cream and then their dinner plans, he had taken his mind off everything that was bothering him earlier. When five o clock was near for him to meet up with his son, Nova's calls went to voicemail. As it became half past five, Keiontay finally took his phone out. He shook his head at the multiple missed call attempts from Nova.

Staring at his phone, he debated on what he should do. He assumed that no matter if unblocked her, called back or texted back, the outcome wouldn't be pretty. To avoid ruining the moment of pure happiness he was having, he turned his phone off completely.

Nova looked around the park hoping she would see Keiontay and her time wouldn't have been wasted. After continuing to call and receiving his voicemail each time, and sitting there for almost two hours, she decided that he wasn't coming. Though her son didn't know about Keiontay coming, he had no expectations. However, she was upset that she did. She had put her faith in him after brushing off her doubts, and it made her angry to feel like her son was reliving a part of her life that she was no fan of. She wanted to scream but, while waiting for Keiontay, Nolan had fallen asleep. So to vent to keep herself from exploding she decided to call her mother who she hadn't spoken to in a while for some motherly advice.

Answering after four rings, her mother answered cheerfully, and that shocked her so that she had to look at the phone to make sure she had called the right number.

"Nova, hey there darling. How are you and my grand baby?"

In search of comfort, Nova started crying as a release of frustration.

"Nova, are you guys okay? Is the baby okay?" her mother asked, trying to figure out what was wrong. "Talk to me, I can't help unless you tell me what's going on."

Trying to calm down enough to speak, she exhaled and said, "Keiontay, he didn't show."

Still lost as to what she was talking about, "huh? I'm not following Nova, we haven't talked in a while honey so I'm lost. What about Keiontay? Are you two back together?"

Pulling herself together, clearing her throat and wiping her tears, she finally said, "Keiontay finally reached out and asked to see Nolan. I agreed to meet him, but he didn't show up. I've been waiting here for almost two hours. And I think he's blocked me."

Her mother started laughing, and instantly Nova got offensive, "what's so funny?" she asked.

"You," her mother stated and continued to laugh until the phone grew silent. "You really believe that boy wants anything to do with either of you. That's the funny part. I really doubt your common sense sometimes. Since I last heard, the man hardly makes any contact with his child, and cut off all communication to him. Now he all of a sudden reaches out, and you believe he's a changed man."

"I never said I thought he was a changed man."

"So what were you thinking then Nova? The man to show up and you three be a happy little family?"

"No, I just.."

"Just what? Again that's why I laughed because the situation is funny. Is that why you called me?"

"I just felt some type of way and it had me thinking about how my dad didn't show up for me, time and time again."

"Girl that baby is not you Nova! He's just getting the hang of walking and is barely talking. You're young enough to find that baby a daddy if you think that's what he needs. Otherwise, life goes the hell on."

"Thank you mom for your comforting words," she said sarcastically.

"I wasn't trying to be comforting. You sitting there crying and comparing your life to a baby's. You sound idiotic," she said and began to laugh again.

No longer in the mood to be insulted, she attempted to switch the subject so that they could soon end the call. "I hear you, so how has everything been with you?" she asked.

"Girl fabulous! I think I might have my foot in the door again so I won't have to work anymore. I met a new guy and I think he's rich, but doesn't want to tell me. I may have hit the jackpot with this one. But we both know, you didn't call in concerns about my personal life. Let's get back to you, Missy. Grow up, all that man did was give you his sperm. If you still want him, you maybe should've further considered the abortion when he asked you. Because it seems like he liked you much better before you got pregnant."

"Wow!" was all Nova could manage to say.

"I'm just saying. It's okay to still be in love with the man, but it's clear he's moved on and neither of you are a priority to him. Dust your feet and move on, child. Just be glad you don't have three and four kids by the man."

Regretting she even called, a text from Omar asking how things were going gave her the momentum she needed to wrap up the call and bring it to an end.

"I honestly regret calling you. For just that minute I needed the person that gave me birth to be on my side. Encourage me, advise me, enlighten me even in this new phase in my life, but that boat sailed right past you. I don't appreciate it, but I see that we're better when we don't talk," Nova stated and waited to see if her mother had anything to say.

"I'm sorry you feel that way because I thought I did a great job of giving you the reality check that you needed."

Laughing slightly, "I'm the one that needed the reality check huh? I hear you, but this conversation no longer needs to be continued. I hope things work out for you with the guy you're trying to get."

"Oh honey, I will get him, there's no ifs ands and buts about it, but get it together Nova. Do better for you and my grandson. You're his mother if you're crying every five seconds, the boy might grow up soft for heaven's sake."

“Okay and on that note for sure, have a good rest of your day,” she said and ended the call before her mother could respond.

As Nova started her car, she headed back home and called Omar on the way. Answering on the first ring,” how did it go?” he asked.

“Well hello to you too and not so good” she said.

“I’m sorry babe,” he said sincerely.

“It’s okay, I just don’t understand why he would make the effort to call and not show.”

“Well first off, it's not okay. I know what it’s like expecting a parent to show up and the disappointment when they don’t feels like. So as a person that’s personally experienced it herself also and trying to give her child what she didn’t have is definitely a let down I can imagine.”

“I had called my mother before calling you and that high key made me feel worse than I did before calling her. She basically laughed at me and questioned my common sense for even going.”

“Damn babe, I see why we get along. I got the toxic father and absent mother, and you got the toxic mother and absent father. Aren’t we a matched pair,” he said and started laughing, causing Nova to laugh some. “But um, that’s fucked up for real though. That’s not what you needed at that moment. You would think that since she was a single mother while raising you she would be a little more understanding."

"Those were my thoughts, but I was terribly mistaken, but we're headed back home. I just want to get in bed, order some food, and pretend like today didn't happen."

Exhaling, "I wish today had gone better. How's Nolan?"

"Luckily he slept mostly through it so he's not phased by anything. He's just back there playing with his toys now and smiling."

"Well that's good, I wish I could come hold you right now, but I have like four more hours on this shift. But dinner is on me, I'll send you something to order you guys dinner tonight."

"Omar, I don't need your money!" she said aggressively.

"Nova, I never said you did. Since I've met you, you were holding it down and I strongly believe you will continue to. I'm not trying to cripple your independence, but help carry the load with you. Plus since I can't be there physically how I know you need me to be. So I figured that's the least I can do."

"I'm sorry, today has just been a lot."

"It's okay, I understand. I promise I'm in your corner. I told you I'm not fucking up my second chance."

Laughing a little, "thank you," she said as his words warmed her heart and made the bumps in the day not seem so hectic.

"You're more than welcome, but I have to go, the truck just came back in and we need to restock it, I'll see you soon."

"Okay, be careful."

"I will, I love you," he said.

Flabbergasted but captivated by him saying the big three words again, she smiled, and said, "I love you too," and the call ended.

Keiontay and Morgan enjoyed their evening out together and agreed to head back to her place to cap off the evening. She suggested a movie and he suggested drinks as the day had been long for him. They agreed to do both. Drink while watching a good movie. They decided to drink cognac and go the comedy route figuring they both needed a good laugh.

Despite the unexpected drama, Morgan was enjoying his company. Feeling free in the moment, the alcohol was giving her some liquid courage. It had been a minute since she had been with somebody and she couldn't deny that she found him attractive. So with the liquid courage invading her veins she had in mind to go for what she wanted at the moment. While she was plotting how to make her move, Keiontay was focused on the movie, waiting to laugh, and just enjoying the chance to relax. With everything going on, to be able to just have a few drinks in a safe environment and watch a good movie was what he needed. It was something he hadn't got a chance to do in a while. Not saying he wasn't appreciative of Morgan, but the way the alcohol was hitting he felt like he was in the room by himself and it felt good.

As a comical scene finally came up, Keiontay started to laugh, but noticed Morgan wasn't paying attention to what was on the screen. He looked over to find her staring at him. Thrown off guard he asked, "are you okay?"

Licking her lips before she spoke, "yeah, I'm great," she said as she continued to look at him.

Laughing slightly, "Your ass drunk I see," he said as he looked at her for a minute then back at the movie.

With no interest to further watch the movie, Morgan wanted to lean in on her curiosities and went with her own vibe unless told otherwise. So she stood up, adjusted her shirt and leggings, and then stood briefly in front of Keiontay before getting on her knees between his legs.

"Yo, what are you doing?" Keiontay asked sitting up trying to close his legs for her to get the hint that that wasn't where his mind was currently.

"Let me just taste you," she pleaded as she lightly rubbed her hand over his manhood.

"Man, get yo drunk ass up talking out your head," he said to deflect her words.

"Keiontay come on. I'm a little intoxicated but you know this has been something that has been building. You feel it, I know you think I'm attractive."

"I'm not saying I don't, this is just unexpected timing."

Feeling in no mood to take no for an answer, she reached into his pants and boxers and started massaging his manhood as she continued to talk, "so that don't feel good?" she asked.

Not pulling away and enjoying her touch, he simply nodded his head and decided to throw caution to the wind and go with the flow. Standing slightly to pull down his pants and boxers, she smiled as he freed his manhood. She was more than ready to help build his erection. Moving in even closer to him, she took his limp manhood and placed the tip on her tongue. She swirled it around before she spit on it and used her hand to stroke his shaft as she french kissed the tip.

Keiontay moaned as he watched her deep throat and stroke his now throbbing erection. Maybe this was something he needed and didn't realize. He was certainly enjoying him self as he found himself beginning to fuck her face. As he held the top of her head, she moaned at the way he was beginning to take charge, it turned her on even more. With her free hand, she reached in her panties and started playing with herself as she continued giving him head.

"Damn," he moaned as he became fixated on her playing with herself. Feeling himself about to cum, he told her to get up. Slightly confused with the desire to finish as she was almost at her own peak, she did as instructed. Keiontay stood up and got behind Morgan, pulled down her pants, panties, and bent her over on the sofa. As he ran his hand over vagina lips before spreading them, he took his erection and inserted himself inside her. Inhaling and moaning simultaneously as he filled her up, she gripped the back of the sofa as he stroked in and out her wetness.

Already on the verge of a built up nut from her oral pleasure, it didn't take much for him to cum. But not before he witnessed Morgan's creamy wetness almost covering his shaft. Smacking her ass as she quivered from cumming, he finally came inside her and felt like the wind had just got knocked out of him. As he caught his breath, he stood there for a minute before he pivoted to the sofa and wiped sweat from his forehead. The nut he had just bust was well needed, but it seemed to awaken the pain of his wounds. Now he was having a small case of regret as it started to feel like pain was shooting through his body. He wanted to take something for pain, but was against mixing anything with the fact he had been drinking.

Morgan was still riding the wave of the alcohol and one of the best orgasms she had just had in her life. As she finally stood up, she pulled up her pants and panties and made it to her bed where she fell asleep almost instantly.

CHAPTER 20

As Ginger followed her initial intuition to go to Tarven's apartment, she saw his car and knew that she was right. She figured it wouldn't take much to get him out of his feelings and things would fall back into place like always. But this time she couldn't be more wrong for the reality check she was about to get.

Knocking on Tarven's door, startling him, he asked who was it and she said, "don't play you already know who this is, now open the door."

He didn't doubt she would put the pieces together. But he had plans to not let her in and to talk to her through the door.

"Tarven, let me in!" she demanded. "I am not about to talk to you through a fucking door!"

Ignoring her and beginning to walk away from the door thinking she would get the hint and leave, she started kicking the door and yelling, "open the fucking door Tarven!" Immediately growing frustrated as he could hear one of his neighbors saying something. Then Ginger and her began to exchange words quickly.

Before things further escalated, he opened the door to Ginger who had gotten in the face of the woman next door. She was threatening to call the police for Ginger disturbing her. Trying to apologize to his neighbor, he pushed Ginger into his apartment, asked his neighbor to forgive her, and closed the door behind them.

"Can you ever fucking act right?" Tarven asked as he looked at Ginger with disgust.

"I wouldn't have to have acted like that if you would have simply just open the fucking door."

"Man whatever Ginger. What do you want?" he asked as he continued to stand by the door.

"You're standing by the door like you don't want me in your damn house, and it's fine. I'll leave your piece of shit, but not without my child, where is she?" she asked, looking around beginning to head towards the bedrooms.

Before she could make it to the first bedroom, where Kaleigh was playing with her toys on the floor, Tareven grabbed her by the arm to stop her.

"What are you doing?" she asked, trying to snatch away from him, but his grip was too tight.

"You're hurting my arm Tarven!" she yelled.

Spinning her around to the door, "I think it's about time you leave. Kaleigh is home and she's safe here with me," he said as he let her arm go. "You don't care about her really. She's always been a pawn to use to get what you want for your own sick pleasure. Not once have you been a mother to her and she doesn't deserve that. A child being in a dysfunctional household is damn near worse than being in a broken one. I refuse to continue letting her witness all the toxicity of her no good of a whore she has for a mother," he yelled.

His words stung Ginger like salt being poured on a wound. She walked up to him and open handedly slapped him. "You're not taking my fucking daughter, what I want to do with her is my fucking choice. I carried her, not you!"

"You haven't even once tried to stop and make sure she's okay, you lied on her, used her, and she's barely fully been in this world for two years."

"This isn't about Kaleigh, you're trying to punish me cause you think I still want Keiontay! And you damn right I do. I never stopped! Just admit you're insecure and jealous, it's okay."

Shaking his head with hate written on his face, "I can't stand you and I refuse to continue to talk to you. I know what you're trying to do and it's not going to work. No matter what you say, you're going home by yourself. Kaleigh is no longer the small responsibility you have to tolerate within your life anymore."

Running past Tarven to the bedroom to find Kaleigh on the floor playing, Ginger picked her up and tried to run past Tarven to the front door, but he caught her by her hair.

"Let me go!" she screamed.

"No!" he yelled. "Put her down Ginger! I'm not playing with you."

"Okay, damn!" she yelled and sat Kaleigh on the ground while Tarven continued to hold her by the head until the baby was fully on the ground.

Once she was down, he let her hair go and slightly pushed her out of the way and went to pick up a crying Kaleigh. "Where were you going with her?" he asked.

"I was going to take her back home with me where she belongs because I am her mother," she stated as she looked at him.

"Just because you give birth, it doesn't make you a mother. How there's sperm donors, there's such a thing as an egg donor, and that's what you were," he said and started to laugh.

"You think that shit funny huh! Well give me back my fucking egg then and I'll do with her what the fuck I please," she yelled and reached for Kaleigh's arms and snatched it forcefully.

Kaleigh let out a loud scream before crying. Tarven had calmed her down, but this cry was one he had never heard before and immediately put his attention on her to figure out what was wrong.

Ginger just looked and still tried to reach for her and instantly focused on her own selfishness despite Kaleigh's screams had him infuriated. He walked and rocked his crying daughter trying to get her to calm down, but she wouldn't so he called 911 with hopes they could help.

Well, he waited and rocked his daughter, Ginger stood there and taunted Tarven about his decision to up and leave with Kaleigh. How all this would have never happened if he had just continued to act as usual when it came to her Keiontay spill.

Shaking his head, her words went in one ear and out the other as he waited to hear sirens. "Ginger, if you hurt this little girl, I swear on my entire existence, you will never see her again and I'm not coming up off that!"

"Oh boo hoo she'll be fine," she said sarcastically.

Hearing the sirens, Tarven dashed to the door to wave down the ambulance and fire engine. As they came rushing up towards him, he immediately started to describe how she wouldn't stop crying. And that he noticed she screamed when her mother snatched her arm too hard.

While the paramedics assessed her it was like everything happened in a split second. The minute the paramedics stated that Kaleigh's elbow seemed to be dislocated and had to be taken to the hospital, Tarven was enraged. As they began to load the two of them into the back of the ambulance, the police arrived. They asked Tarven if everything was okay, and he told them no and he wanted Ginger removed from his property.

Taking the order and following his request, they entered the house to escort Ginger out, but she refused to leave willingly. She tried to fight them at first but they ended up tasering her to calm her down. As Tarven and Kaleigh rode away in the ambulance, Tarven watched as Ginger was being put in handcuffs in the back of the police car.

As they asked her name and ran her information. "It looks like today is our lucky day. It says here that you have a warrant for your arrest for probation violation," the officer stated. He began to read her rights and let her know they were taking her in to be processed. And that she would also be charged with disorderly conduct.

With Tarven and Ginger dealing with their new fates of life, Omar was wrapping up his shift and thinking of what's next for him in his life. When he talks to Nova, he finds peace even in her hardships, he never wants to stray away, and her smile alone makes his day. The thought of how he was standing in his own way, almost led him to losing the best woman he has ever met had him thinking about risking it all.

He felt that they had already wasted so much time and wanted to show her how serious he was about finally accepting that she was his one. With him uttering the words "I love you" had him feeling stronger than ever and like he was on top of the world. He had encountered plenty of women before, but never one he was deeply in love with. Nova didn't know, but he figured that one day soon he would tell her that she was his first true love. Everyone before was practice and a stepping stone in the development of the man he is today. He had doubts on ever truly accepting that true love was possible. When the first woman that was supposed to love him, roamed the world freely with no thoughts of even checking on him.

So Nova meant more to him than she even realized and him too. Even with her son Nolan, he felt himself wanting to be there for him every step of the way. Be that male role model he needs.

How Omar was on the verge of wanting to flip his entire life around, let him know that he was in a different stage in his life. It was new and nothing he had never encountered before, but he was loving it. Of course he noticed other women, but compared to Nova, nobody else could hold a candle to her. He enjoyed spending time with her, their dates, the way they could find humor in the smallest of things, and most importantly how they could talk about anything. She was the best friend he always needed, and he needed her to know how he felt. He wasn't sure how to express it all as this was a first time for him, but he decided to just follow his instincts.

As the ten hour shift came to an end and the sunrise adorned the sky, instead of heading home to shower like usual after a long day, he had another plan in mind. He drove to the closest Walmart and waited for it to open so he could go in and follow through with his impulsive yet thoughtful items he had in mind. Rushing in the store like he was trying to beat a crowd, he grabbed a cart, sprinted to the flowers. Grabbed three bouquets of red roses, some grey and white memory foam house shoes, and a gift bag. Then headed to the jewelry department and purchased a ten karat white gold key pendant necklace.

More than satisfied with his choices, he headed towards the check out, but ended up making a beeline to the toy department as he thought about Nolan. His plan was to make sure he was included with what he had in mind. Not fully sure what he was into, he went with his heart and picked him out an inflatable ball pit. With the hope that he would like it, he proceeded to check out, and loaded his car with his purchase. He stopped at Starbucks to grab them breakfast and headed to Nova's apartment. Praying all his hard work would not go in vain.

With him knowing that Nova was an early bird, he knew she would be up doing her usual morning routine. His intentions were to make it to her before Nolan woke up, but either way it would be okay. As he arrived, he was filled with nerves. He started to think if she said no today how he would be understanding, but truly disappointed. Before he talked himself out of all the ways it could go wrong or what excuse she would give, he exhaled, looked to the sky, and headed to her front door.

Knocking on the door, he waited for her to open the door as he heard nothing. He wanted it to be a surprise, but was hesitant about showing up unannounced. Starting to overthink everything and wondering if she was even at home, he contemplated turning around. Letting fear of the unknown and the immediate answer to unexpected knocks, he started to walk away from her door. Instantly feeling almost defeated, he took a minute to look around the parking lot to see if she was even home before he jumped to conclusions. The minute he finally spotted her car, he heard a door open, but didn't look back because he figured it was probably one of the neighbors.

"Omar," Nova said as she had finally come to the door and noticed him walking away.

Turning around with a slight smile on his face, "Hey," he said, beginning to approach her.

"You got your hands full there," she said, noticing the roses, gift bag, Starbucks, and toy box.

"I do. Can I come in?" he asked as he stood and looked at her.

"Of course," she said as she stepped to the side. "I wasn't expecting you this morning. I figured you would be heading home by now."

"I usually do, but something came to mind. Plus I didn't feel right going home without checking on you knowing the day you guys had."

"That's sweet, but it made you buy me flowers?" she asked.

"Not exactly, this is for something completely different actually," he stated.

"Oh really?"

As he went and sat on the sofa, Nova joined him on the opposite side and tried to help him unload everything but he refused.

"Everything I'm holding right now has meaning, and I need to explain it before I ask what I truly want."

"Ohhh okay," she said, starting to feel nervous now.

"Well, here's a vanilla caramel latte for you and two breakfast sandwiches. I was hoping I could make it here before you cooked breakfast so you wouldn't have to."

"Okay, thank you and I actually hadn't started yet. I was in the bathroom when you first knocked, which is what took me so long," she said and laughed slightly.

"Ah, gotcha," he said, starting to laugh as he understood what she was saying without actually saying it. "Ok, so, secondly here's some roses, because I just wanted to make you smile. And let you know I was that you really mean more to me than I ever realized. So I figured roses would be a good way of showing that."

"That I love you from earlier caught me off guard because for the longest I've longed to hear those words leave your mouth for me. I know you said it before but then I thought maybe you were just going with the moment, but then, just wow. I used to dream about what it would sound like, so to finally hear it still got me a little giggly."

"Giggly? Okay, but man Nova you got fucked up for real. Not in a bad way, but in a way I don't recognize about myself. Like I know I said it before, but in life second chances get rarer by the minute. You could've easily written me off, but you heard me out and trusted me to prove myself. I can't lie, for a minute I was upset about you moving on at first. But I understood because you did deserve better than how I was treating you. So now is my chance to treat you how you should've been treated. Giving you the appreciation you deserve because you are more than your body. You're beautiful, you're intelligent, you're ambitious, a hell of a Mother, independent, nurturing, selfless, and so much more. I still want to kick my own ass for not realizing your worth sooner. So every chance I get to remind you of how appreciative I am, I am going to show you."

Tearing up slightly as she was captivated by his words, she could only smile as she wanted to see where this was all going.

"I know you're wondering where all this is going, but here's the second part of why I'm here," he said as he reached in the gift bag and pulled out the pair of house shoes.

"Those look comfy and I did need a new pair," she said.

"Why the gift of a pair of house shoes you wonder?"

"Exactly my thoughts," she said.

"Well, yes they are regular house shoes, but I want these house shoes to be a manifestation to the house we find to be our home. When you've had a long day or simply get off work, these can be a pair of your go to shoes."

"Aw that's so sweet and I love that you see a future for us. That's nice to hear."

"I'm glad you feel that way," he said as he handed her the gift bag.

She opened the bag and pulled out a gift box to reveal the pendant necklace shaped like a key. She was mesmerized at the diamonds and the gift in general. "I love it! Thank you, I can't wait to wear it," she said, smiling from ear to ear.

"Before you take it out the box, I want you to know that I selected that particular necklace for two reasons. One because Nova Emerson, you are the first woman in this world to help me grow up without realizing it...like you moving on let me know that I needed to get my shit together and there was more to life than just being sexual. I had my own dreams, but the opportunity to just let me be and accept that I'm working on me is something I appreciate so much. Because of that time, I also noticed I finally trusted and found love. You just being you helped me believe in love finally. So one meaning is corny, but you have the key to my heart, and secondly, call me crazy, but it also is my way of asking for us to move in together? But not into either of our apartments, but to find a place we both like. The three of us."

Speechless as she wiped tears from her eyes. She felt like she was definitely dreaming as it seemed to be moving so fast.

"I don't have any money saved to move right now and maybe you're just stuck in the moment. We're a lot to take on every day. So maybe you should re-think what you're asking Omar."

“First off, I never asked you for a dime. The goal is to find something we both like, and I’ll handle the financial aspect of things. The place will be in both of our names so there’s no feeling like this is just my place but truly ours. The other stuff, we can work through, but initially, the question is, are you in? What are your thoughts?” he stated and waited nervously for her response.

“Umm, this is big,” she said as she stared at the necklace trying to process what it all now meant.

“I overdid it huh?” he asked, starting to regret his choice to be impulsive and follow what he was feeling. “I came on too strong,” he added. He turned from Nova and looked forward as he prepared himself for the rejection he was afraid he would get.

“I once heard that you can’t want love again, and not be willing to trust letting it happen. A part of healing is stepping out there and not holding you at fault for what was. I don’t have any comparisons to make because not even every Monday or Tuesday, Wednesday and so forth are the same. The days of the week may remain the same, but no day or week are similar. I know that was a lot of rambling kind of, but umm, yes.”

Shocked at the answer he heard, he turned and looked at her with a smile he didn’t intend to have, but was glad it was happening.

Filled with excitement, he pulled her to him and they hugged for about a minute just cherishing the moment and the new step they were about to take.

"Man this is crazy," she said, coming out of their embrace.

"I know, but you guys are worth it and I don't want life without either of you. If anything, I want to be able to enhance your life. I just hate it took me so long to realize it," he stated.

"You never know what will happen in life for God to align you where he truly wants you to be," she responded as she looked at him.

"I can feel that."

"I have a confession to make since you shared something very personal. I don't regret my son because he is one of the best things that has ever happened to me. But I wish I had learned to be more patient and more expressive of my feelings when it came to you and I initially. Everything does happen for a reason and despite the hell I have been through, it taught me how to stand up for myself, be expressive, and understand effective communication with my partner is important. Even helped me learn to be a little more patient. Hell though it was like my storm in a sense, it helped to mature us both."

"Very true because I never would have probably realized what I was about to lose."

"True, but umm what's up with the toy box?" she asked, starting to laugh.

"Well it was like a little symbolism for Nolan too. In hopes he would like it, it would go well in his bedroom in our new place. I wanted to include him too basically. I didn't want to get him jewelry, but something fun in a sense."

"Ah I gotcha, that is truly sweet of you. I thank you so much for thinking of him. Like no offense, that probably means more to me than any of this. Because I know there's plenty of men that have stepped up to be great Dads to kids that aren't theirs. I just had a little disbelief of if I would ever have my turn. I know my son deserves that level of guidance that I can't give him," said she and started to tear up.

CHAPTER 21

Walking into the living room to where Keiontay was on the sofa scrolling through his phone, “Good morning,” Morgan said as she walked past him to the kitchen.

“Good morning,” he said back as he stayed fixated on his phone.

Coming back out of the kitchen with a bottle of water, “I thought I would wake up with you next to me,” she said as she sat next to him on the sofa.

Adjusting himself and moving away slightly, “naw, you were passed out pretty much when I got up to go to the bathroom. Plus why would I do that?” he asked.

“I mean I don’t fully remember everything about last night, but I know we did have sex and it was pretty good. So I just thought you might have wanted to sleep in the bed with me or now felt that you could.”

“Oh, umm, naw I still wanted to give you your space, plus I was in pain for a great part of the night that sobered me up pretty quickly. But umm, I’ve been waiting for you to get up so we can go to the store. So can we head to the store right quick before you get your day started?” he asked.

“Wait, in pain, oh shit, I forgot. I was just in the moment and wasn’t truly expecting you to even take over like that, but I am sorry that you were in pain. And umm what do you need from the store, I can order it and have it brought to the house.”

“Yeah no, this is a pressing matter. Fuck it, I’m going to pay for it, but we need to go buy a plan b because I don’t think I pulled out last night. Outside of my pain last night the nightmares of you being pregnant had me tossing and turning. So can we please go get one for you to take before it's too late?”

“Wow, what a great way to start my day. Yeah we can, but damn me being pregant by you would be a nightmare that’s fucked up,” she said and stood up. “I open my home to you and am basically supporting you, but more than that and I’m got damn freddy krueger.”

“Morgan, I’m not saying it like that honestly. The nightmare is I haven’t had the best success with being a father. I just don’t feel ready for another child right now honestly. It has nothing to do with you, it’s me and not even on no cliche shit, like being legit.”

“I mean I can get it, but its the way you said it that’s fucked up,” she said and walked in her bedroom and threw on some clothes so they could go to the store.

As she walked back in the living room ready to go, she still had an attitude at the way things went. Because her hopes for the morning were to have a positive conversation about what was next for them. As far as a possible title with the fact of him moving to Texas with her and them just having sex. But his delivery about their night of passion had Morgan thinking and feeling like Keiontay was just using her and wasn't truly interested in her.

"I can buy my own plan b. Save whatever money you have. You can stay here if you want and I'll just go," she said as she stood by the door.

"Morgan, why the attitude?" he asked, picking up that there was something wrong with her.

"Nothing, I can just buy my own shit. Simple. I don't need you to go with me. Oh you must think I'm not going to take it? Trust and believe, I am because I definitely wouldn't want to be stuck with nobody that doesn't want to be. So you don't have to worry about that," she stated as she grabbed her keys and opened the door to leave.

Exhaling and putting his phone down, "Morgan, I know my delivery was wrong but you took this the wrong way. This is a me thing, my life is not together enough for another child. As a man I made the mistake of not pulling out, so it is my responsibility to be accountable for my actions. So that involves my money, not yours. I don't doubt for a damn minute you can get it yourself, but let me handle what I did," he said as he stood up.

Morgan said nothing further and let Keiontay ride to the store with her. The ride to cvs was silent at first outside of the radio until Keiontay broke the silence.

"Before we leave for Texas, I tracked down my car. I want to go get it so I can sell it. I can have some extra money and be able to contribute to the move. I know you have pretty much everything handled, but I'm sure I was not a part of the original plans. It won't take long for the car to sell honestly. Plus it'll be like me starting over all together and I need that."

"Well thank you for thinking of me in that sense and wanting to help out. I appreciate it because for a minute there I was starting to think...." she began to say but he finished her sentence.

"That I was just trying to use you, no I'm not. Before I met you, I had plans to leave anyway but the situation set me back. So I'm more grateful than you know to have somebody to actually start over with. I couldn't have met a better woman that's so patient and understanding," he expressed.

As they pulled into the parking lot of the store, Morgan inhaled and exhaled as she looked at him. "Man you're a charmer for sure," she said and started laughing.

"I'm a little smooth here and there, but not for real. I do like you and I know I have my problems, but I wouldn't mind seeing where things go when we get to Texas."

"Oh really," she said as she started to get out of the car.

Focused on getting what they came for, the conversation came to a halt as they went in, found it, grabbed a water for her, a gatorade for him, checked out, and came back out. Morgan wasted no time in cracking the package open, taking the pill out, putting it in her mouth and swallowing it with water.

She stuck out her tongue and lifted it to show she took it as she wanted to stay on course for her career. She was never against it, she just didn't like the way he had initially said it, but that was behind them. What he didn't expect is what was about to come next.

Morgan asked where the car was and if he wanted to go and get the car today. Happy she was willing to go today he disclosed the name of the junkyard it had been dropped off to.

Shocked by his response of the given name, "Whattt? What a small world for real. That's my Uncle's place. He owns it but doesn't work there much. I still to this day don't know what else he does, but since I have been alive that junkyard has been around I know," she stated.

"Definitely a small world," he said as he looked at his phone thinking about how a part of him wanted to keep his car. But realized that if he could let go of it, the rewards would be greater. So he put his mind to ease and just chunked it all up as a way to do better for himself.

"I don't even need the address to know how to get there. In fact, I hope my uncle is there because I haven't seen him in a while," she said as they began to leave the parking lot to head to the junkyard. Making small talk on the way there led to Morgan saying, "you might have met him and not even realize it. My uncle is real down to Earth and will help anybody. He's just an overall good guy. I call him Uncle Kai for short, but his name is Malachi."

Keiontay's face grew worried instantly as he started to think that maybe he had been sat up. Quickly dismissing his thoughts as he realized she was talking about him as if they hadn't spoken in a while. To test his assumption to see if he was about to have to swarm his way out of moving with her if that was the case, he asked, "when was the last time you talked to your uncle?"

"Oh wow, umm it's been a minute. We're not as close as we used to be. For a while when I was younger, we were tied at the hip. He was like a second Dad for me, but he started to date different women that took his attention. As I got older, nursing school took up a lot of my time, and I guess after a while our communication just drifted apart. Maybe that's why you were put in my life, to help reconnect me with my uncle."

"Oh okay," he said dryly as he processed her words and led to confirm that she had nothing to do with what Malachi did to him.

Excited to take the drive with the hope to reunite with her Uncle she wasn't noticing Keiontay's now distance and change of attitude. "Hey, you mind if we put off going today? I'm kind of having second thoughts," he said, beginning to fabricate a lie as he spoke.

"Wait? Why, the change of heart,"she asked as she looked at him but tried to keep her eyes on the road.

"I just thought the guy that had reached out to me to buy the car was legit. He fell through and the other person that had reached out never responded back to me at all. So I don't want to bother getting it and it's just sitting in front of your place and we're about to leave in less than two weeks."

With disappointment apparent in her voice, "ah man, um well okay, that does make sense. I don't want to be charged for an abandoned car. Dang, I guess I'll just reach out to my uncle one of these days when I get a chance."

"Thank you for being understanding," he said feeling relieved that he dodged that bullet that could have been more literal than just metaphorically.

"What a roller coaster ass morning," she laughed and said and Keiontay nodded his head in agreement.

"Well, I'm hungry and I'm going to make myself some breakfast and if you want some I don't mind sharing," she said as they arrived back to her place.

"I would appreciate that honestly because I am starving honestly. When I'm able to move around without these damn crutches as much, I'm making you breakfast in bed. With some other stuff for you coming through for me like you've known me for years."

"I hope you're a man of your word, but before we go in this house I didn't forget. You said you wouldn't mind if things went further and," she started to say and intentionally didn't finish her statement to let him fill in what he was saying before they got out of the car.

"Yes, I am a man of my word and I wasn't just talking. I do like you and let's not act like I can forget the way that thing was talking to me last night," he said and started laughing that made her laugh.

"I heard it for sure," she said in between laughing. "But that doesn't complete what you were about to say."

"Hell, I forgot now. I probably need to eat and then we can further discuss it, I promise."

With plenty more to figure out besides just where they stood, Morgan felt more comfortable about taking this next step with a man she now no longer viewed as a stranger, but somebody she was falling for. He came with plenty of baggage, but she saw him in a different light of being more so misunderstood than him coming with so much. With the desire to live the so-called half ass American dream of having a great career, living in a great neighborhood, being married, kids, a white picket fence, and a dog.... She felt she was on the road to living the dream, but was short of a couple of things. But with Keiontay now being in her life, she saw potential in this man that had entered her life at an unprecedented time.

Morgan felt she had been given lemons at first but she was learning how to quickly turn those lemons into pound cake. Though she saw the light in Keiontay there was still some darkness he was lucky to have swept under the rug for now. How long it would stay under wraps was the question that neither of them knew.

As for Keiontay, he was starting to truly like Morgan more than just a person to help him transition into this new chapter of his life. He liked the fact that she was drama free, was about her business, and didn't pry too much into his past. She accepted him now for who he was and went from there, but he couldn't help to see a lot of Nova in Morgan. In being honest with himself he was moving to Texas with another woman, but was still in love with Nova. The problem he saw was trying to find his way back to her, and the minute he heard Omar's voice he believed the point of expressing his true feelings were pointless. So for his new start whether he was ready or not he had in mind to convince himself to fall for Morgan. He felt Nova didn't deserve to have her life on pause while he figured out his life. Though he wished she had. Her waiting could have been the key to him sticking around a little longer.

Though Morgan was getting the short end of the stick, that was something he vowed to carry to his grave for however long it turned out for him and her. Plus, he saw telling her would only make her feel insecure and question his intentions which is something he didn't need. As for his son, he prayed that one day he would be able to face him and be able to confess why he wasn't a part of his life much. A part of him felt like a coward, but he felt it was hard to rebuild what he destroyed with his immaturity.

Over the days of last minute doctor visits, helping Morgan pack, gathering the few items he had, Keiontay prepared to put Georgia behind for the first time in his life. All he had ever known was the state of Georgia. It was the place he was born, raised, grew up in, first job, first fell in love, had his first child, been through plenty of hell, and more. It was always his only home, maybe different cities across the state, but predominantly it was home. Everywhere he only visited, but on the verge of being a Texan, it was his reset. A part of him felt bad for not not showing up to see Nolan one last time. Aside from Nova not knowing about his injuries, the truth was seeing Nova was harder for him than he realized. To see her he would have the desire for things to fall into place like a fairytale and he knew that wasn't possible. Along with the fact of still living on the thought of feeling rejected when she asked for healing. He knew it was only right what she was saying, but her not jumping to welcome him back with open arms had a part of him angry and desiring to be spiteful.

He planned to go about his life and one day, Nova would see him being happy and regret destroying what they could have had. At least that's how he felt it should be. The truth of knowing that he was wrong was a truth he found more comfort in lying about instead.

8 WEEKS LATER

Keiontay and Morgan were now official residents of Texas and they were starting to settle in quite finely. Keiontay was off of his crutches and rehab was going great. It was to the point where he was almost back to being fully mobile on his own. He started doing some freelance work in engineering to bring in some income, and Morgan was working as a nurse at one of the top hospitals in the state. In his mind, the decision to move was better than he thought. Though he wished it was Nova and Nolan he had made this big decision with, he was happy with the way things were going.

He even kept his promise of cooking Morgan breakfast in bed once he got better and she was shocked he could cook. He was truly developing a strong liking of her but there times when they had sex he would imagine it was Nova or while they were out sworn he seen Nova.

“I wish letting her go was as easy as this move was,” is something Keiontay said constantly when he would have episodes of missing Nova. Some nights, going outside on the balcony of their two bedroom apartment was when he found the time and safe place to shed a tear of the pain he felt from missing the two people in the world that had his heart most. The reminders of either of them made the pain sometimes unbearable where he found himself at times snapping at Morgan. But instead of confessing that his frustration came from him still being in love with Nova and him missing his son, he would lie and say it was just work related.

When his parents called to check in on him, he pretended that everything was good and that he had gotten his life together. That he had gotten a job opportunity in Texas which is why he all of a sudden moved there without telling them he was leaving the state. Yes, a great part of his life was now him living a web of lies that he was weaving at any indication of the truth of how he really ended up in Texas. Even when Morgan started to ask about meeting his family one day, he gave the excuse of work deadlines and still wanting to get settled into Texas.

But what he didn't know was that he wasn't the only one withholding the truth. Morgan had her own truth she was keeping from Keiontay and a secret that she would take to her grave. About two weeks into moving to Texas and the first full week of working at her new job she got sick. She thought nothing of it until she was midway through a shift, found herself light headed and having to cut her shift short. One of her co-workers joked that if she knew her better she would think that maybe she had just had a long day and maybe hadn't eaten or was stressed out, but since she didn't know her while it just seemed like pregnancy symptoms to her. As that coworker joked, it sent off an alert in Morgan's head that she hadn't got her period. Between packing in Georgia, moving here, getting unpacked, finding places, getting adjusted to her work schedule, it hadn't crossed her mind. When they went shopping for cleaning supplies she couldn't remember going to the feminine care aisle for nothing in the world.

Based on her connecting the dots of dates and the way she was feeling, she ended up taking a pregnancy test and it came back positive. In her working in a hospital it wasn't hard for her to get her questions asked on how and why this was possible. The minute the test came back she took the first appointment an obgyn had available to see if this test was legit. It was accurate, she was pregnant. Six weeks to be exact.

Confused on how that was possible when she took a plan b in the allotted time frame before 72 hours. The doctor explained that though the emergency contraceptive is effective, it does have side effects that could cause the pill to not be as effective. She explained that if her body had already started ovulating that the pill wouldn't have been effective. With her body already ovulating and him ejaculating inside of her, the egg had been fertilized.

Morgan was well aware of the steps it took to get pregnant, but she was sure she had dodged that bullet that day. And from then on every time after they had sex Keiontay made sure to pull out or she let him come in her mouth. So there was no worry until the two red lines boldly stared back at her, and the words of the doctor telling her she was indeed pregnant. A great bit of women usually are excited to count down the months to bring life into this world, but for Morgan it was a curve ball of news that she wasn't ready to be excited about. So before the doctor could ask or give any further information or suggestions for prenatal care, Morgan asked to be given the abortion pill.

Throughout the whole ordeal, Morgan not once said anything to Keiotay about the pregnancy. When the pill took on some of its side effects of bleeding and cramping, he paid it no mind and just thought she was on her period and she didn't correct him. When he noticed her bleeding for a little longer than most females, he asked if she should go to the hospital and he would go with her, but she lied and said it was just the stress of everything. So for the first few weeks in Texas, they outwardly were happy to be in a new state and adjusting well. Internally they were at war with lies that were eating at them. And the saddest part is that neither of them had plans to come clean. For him, according to her, he was slowly falling for her which was far from the truth. As for her, he would never know that she chose her career and new beginning over letting him be a part of the decision of the child they had created.

****

Tarven and Ginger had finally called it quits for good. From the day everything went down, Tarven gave all of his focus to being the best Father he could be to Kaleigh. The night he got back from the hospital with her from the incident, it was determined that Ginger had given her a nursemaid. Luckily by going the same day it happened, the doctor was able to pop it back in place and send her home with splint and sling for about a week and a half.

For Tarven that was good news that she would be okay, but that moment was a long overdue reality check for him. He had finally cashed out on the fact that not all forms of love are worth fighting for. No matter the amount of times he tried to fight for Ginger, it was never good enough. He was losing himself more so than becoming a better version of himself. How he treated Ginger had him doing some self reflecting. If karma ever came around and bit him in the ass by giving his daughter a guy like him how he was to Ginger he wouldn't be pleased.

It was heartbreaking for him to cut ties with her, even when she tried to call collect, he blocked her before he changed his number all together. Then he followed through on moving into a bigger apartment, changing Kaleigh's daycare, and fighting for full custody over his daughter. However, with Ginger's record and serving time at the moment, there wasn't much of a custody battle. The judge granted Tarven full custody with no problem.

There were times he wanted to take Kaleigh to visit her or put money on her books. But he knew if he helped at any point or showed there was still love for her, she would work her way back into his life. And he had to be stronger than that, not just for the sake of their daughter and court orders, but himself as well. To be in a relationship like that was unhealthy and draining. In further pursuit to be a better version of himself, he started going to therapy once a week. He found joy in being able to have someone to help him process what he was going through, had gone through, and how to best deal with everything.

Then despite not knowing where he was exactly and he was okay with that, Keiontay and Tarven became good friends again. Maybe not a talk on the phone everyday or the type of brotherhood they used to have, but they both found comfort in familiarity in their chapters of new beginnings.

Ginger, that's a different story....all of her hell finally caught up with her and the judge was done giving her the benefit of a doubt. When it came time for her hearing, the judge had seen her face one too many times, and sentenced her to three years in Fulton County Jail for probation violation and disorderly conduct. With the chance to be paroled in two years with ankle monitoring. Most people would see jail as their freedom being taken away, but for once in her life she felt like she had finally reached the end of her rope. She had gone as far as she could go in demanding and taking her way from people. She initially was never afraid of jail and still wasn't because she knew when she made it there it was because she had destroyed her own chances and had nobody to blame. There was nothing or no one for her to look forward to getting out to. About her first month into her sentence, she was served. Where she was being informed that her rights to Kaleigh had been revoked and that Tarven had full custody. Her hunt for Keiontay was now cold. As all of her work was now locked away until whenever she was released. The only way she could now keep up with him was stalking his social media.

Her biggest regret was that she got so close, but wasn't able to follow through to get the one man she loved most. She hated that he saw her as more of an enemy than the love she was trying to give him. In her mind she was no monster, she just never was shown love properly and only defined it the way she taught herself. To her, the way she loved was her normalcy and everybody else was wrong. But in reaching the end of the road she would have continued to travel it, even though it was leading nowhere. Now she was able to focus on the healing she long ago needed since she was fourteen years old. Her held secrets of things done to her became the destruction of not only herself, but the lives of others as well.

While she counted down the days to her freedom, she started counseling but quickly stopped as she didn't see herself progressing. Instead solidarity, and stories of other inmates helped transform her. Listening to the reason why some of them were there had her finally feeling ashamed and regretful for the way she had been acting. In becoming close with her cell mate that was in jail for aggravated assault for up to twenty years, made her say damn. When she disclosed that she happily shot her boyfriend who broke up with her because he wanted to move on but she didn't, had Ginger ready to judge. As she told the story, she laughed through it mostly and stated that she was abiding by the code of if she couldn't have him, nobody else could.

In listening to her, Ginger determined that her cell mate needed much help. Then did some self reflection and noticed that she was pointing the finger, but wasn't much better herself.

"It took me having to lose everything I ever worked to get and thought I wanted to finally work on finally growing up. Admitting that I should have never let my past mold me into a person that people saw as a monster," she thought to herself for almost the first three months of her sentence. She wrote that statement over and over until she could start writing down and confessing the truths she had long ago buried in her mind. She cried through most of it and even landed herself in the psychic ward a time or two from two attempted suicides.

But contrary to belief, jail saved her life and gave her the new beginning she needed. A fresh start where she focused on first forgiving herself, learning to love herself and continuing to heal before taking on other things. Including being a Mother and she was okay with that. Her goals when she got out was to continue to do some outpatient counseling, find her a one bedroom apartment, and expand her past time of art. In art, she discovered a way to express herself more positively.

****

Nova & Omar took elevation to another level. From the day he asked for them to move in together, it's like they grew closer and worked on healing together in ways they didn't both know they needed. She got a chance to meet his siblings and that was different for her to be with someone who had siblings that were inviting. They took to her and Nolan very quickly and that meant a lot to Nova.

Omar helped Nova to understand that when it came to Keiontay that she had to accept what he was giving her or more so their son at the moment, and not to blame herself. Accept that she was doing her best as a Mother and she had good intentions to show up that day in effort to let him know that he was still welcomed, but it was him that missed out. He helped her to not be angry and be willing to be open to the day when he decided to reach out again when he built the nerve. Even if it never happened any time soon to still at least keep her mind open to the possibility. And know that Nolan was their only common denominator.

In listening to Omar's words of encouragement and working on forgiving herself for things that she let happen to her, she grew more into the woman she always knew she could one day be.

While the house search was stressful, finding their ideal house fit for the three of them, and spending time at each other's place helping one another pack up their belongings was a bonding moment they needed. She got a chance to see pictures of him as a kid, pictures of his mother, what life was like for him growing up, high school pictures and the same for him with Nova. They had simple disagreements here and there, but nothing that didn't help develop them. And his family revealed to Nova that seeing them together is the happiest they had ever seen their brother since they could remember. They appreciated her for that and were happy to know her.

"Hopefully, you'll be a part of the family real soon," Omar's sister said one day as they had brunch together.

Laughing it off, Nova thought nothing more of it as she was happy to feel like her life was finally coming together with less tears of sadness, frustration, and drama. And more smiles and tears of joy than she could have ever imagined.

In the midst of house hunting, her birthday was nearing and celebrating was the last thing on her list. As she focused on getting them a place and away from all the clutter that now filled both their living rooms. Omar refused to let her not celebrate, so he surprised with a romantic dinner and the gift of keys to an office space he rented for her to start the business she had been loaning for.

Speechless with shock that he had remembered and heard her dreams she had told him, she kissed him, but suddenly grew sad and started to cry.

Thinking it was because of his surprise, he told her, "Nova, baby you don't have to cry, I know it's a little much, but I just want you to know that I hear you. I support you, I believe in you, and hope to be with you every step of the way."

As Nova wiped her tears, she cleared her throat before she spoke, "you've been so good to me. You helped be my shield for someone who I didn't know how to handle, but was tired of. I never went to my family because as you can tell they're not the most level headed, good people that a person should have. So the way you handled the situation with maturity gave me a calmness that I wasn't sure how to get to. The way your siblings accept me and my son make me feel so included..” she started to say before Omar cut her off fearing that the conversation was about to go left.

“Nova, do you no longer want to move in together?” he asked.

“Man, are you crazy? With all this damn packing we have done, your ass stuck with us!” she laughed.

Smiling, but feeling confused, “then why the look of fear on your face or like something is wrong,” he said as he grabbed her hand. “Your hands are shaking Nova, what’s wrong?” he inquired. “Just spit it out.”

“My first time having to say this didn’t go well. We have agreed to help each other deal with the things we have been through. Admitted that certain things will take longer to heal from than most, as healing is not an overnight process.”

“True,” he said as he waited for her to finish.

“Well, okay, I’m going to say it and just let it play out however it should. Then deal with it that way.”

“Nova, what are you talking about?”

“Omar, I’m pregnant,” she confessed and dropped her head and started crying.

With her head dropped she didn’t notice the smile that had emerged on Omar’s face, “that’s what’s been bothering you?” he asked, causing her to look up.

"Yeah because I didn't know how you would feel about it, and I was unfortunately thinking the worst based on my last experience. Kids are something we've never really talked about outside of you being there for Nolan. Other than that, that's a subject we haven't touched."

He intertwined his fingers with hers, but before he could speak, she cut him off, "Before you say what you feel, I know it might not be fair but I apologize in advance, but I'm keeping my child. It might be weird living together but if this is where we have to end then fine. I'm not getting rid of my baby."

"Girl hush, and you damn right you keeping our baby the hell. What you thought this was? Oh, you thought I was going to be mad or not excited? Because you're all the way wrong, that shit just made my day. I just want the chance to relive the moment of you finding out. Like I've never experienced such a moment. So I can go buy a test. I want it for my memories too," he expressed.

Shocked by Omar's words and excitement, Nova felt like she was truly getting a second chance and the dream she always wanted.

Aside from closing on their new construction five bedroom all brick home, they were counting down the weeks to the arrival of their baby girl Olivia. Nova didn't know it, but for Omar, she had answered a doubt that he could make children. Because in all his years, he hadn't even once encountered a scare. Not that he was trying, but just didn't know he could have kids. But he failed to realize that a great bit of things are based on the right timing.

This is why while watching Nova carry the life they both created, he admired how she was handling things well. From furnishing the house, her business soaring, keeping Nolan a priority, making sure he was happy and incorporating more prayer in their life, to still managing to keep herself up. He knew that there was a pear shaped white gold diamond band ring that had her name all over it. As he wanted not just his daughter to carry on his last name but Nova and Nolan too.

His dream of creating the family he always wanted was finally coming true. Breaking generational curses before them might not have been possible, but they were on the road to giving their kids something neither of them had ever experienced. They both were anxious, but looked forward to life as the Russell family.

More books by Author Vallean J.

Love On Thin Ice

A jaw dropping love story that leads to unexpected betrayal and love used as a weapon. As the paths of Nova Emerson and Keiontay Clark continue to cross, Nova thought that fate was showing its hand in her life and she had finally encountered her one true love.But as Nova drops the guard of her heart, she starts to question her decision to be in a relationship with so many red flags. The urge to have to look over her shoulder starts to become second nature. Someone has made Nova their target, and this obsession is jeopardizing her success and life. Pushed past her limits, Nova is stuck in the crossfire of love and hate.Is Keiontay really her forever — or will his past and decisions become her achilles heel?

Love On Thin Ice

2-Exposed

The drama continues to unravel in this love story and exposes some dark truths that change lives and reveal true intentions.

With the gunshot leaving behind an open wound, revenge becomes the agenda for the unexpected duo to get the ultimate payback. Tarven shows his hand that crosses the lines of friendship, and while Nova has been on a roller coaster when it comes to her love for Keiontay, he is now in the crossfire of finding his own identity.

Will love fix the damage caused by the exposure of love and friendship, or become everyone's downfall?

Follow her on social media:

Facebook, Instagram, TikTok, Twitter, & YouTube

@authorvalleanj

Made in the USA
Columbia, SC
20 October 2023